She'd Forgotten How Tender A Kiss Could Be, How Sweet.

Tears filled her eyes. She realized now how badly she'd wanted his kiss, how long she'd yearned for his touch.

As if sensing her need, he drew her closer. Heat spilled through her as he deepened the kiss, holding her body against his. Each place his body touched hers tingled with awareness.

Much too soon, he withdrew and she opened her eyes to find his gaze on her. Lifting a hand, he swept a thumb beneath her eye, catching a tear that had escaped.

"I'm sorry. I didn't mean to upset you."

"No," she said. "You didn't upset me. It's just that I—"

She dropped her gaze, unable to tell him that the tears were tears of joy, not anger or hurt. But the feelings were too unexpected, too confusing to share.

And the secrets she'd kept were too long hidden to reveal....

Dear Reader,

As expected, Silhouette Desire has loads of passionate, powerful and provocative love stories for you this month. Our DYNASTIES: THE DANFORTHS continuity is winding to a close with the penultimate title, *Terms of Surrender*, by Shirley Rogers. A long-lost Danforth heir may just have been found—and heavens, is this prominent family in for a big surprise! And talk about steamy secrets, Peggy Moreland is back with *Sins of a Tanner*, a stellar finale to her series THE TANNERS OF TEXAS.

If it's scandalous behavior you're looking for, look no farther than *For Services Rendered* by Anne Marie Winston. This MANTALK book—the series that offers stories strictly from the hero's point of view—has a fabulous hero who does the heroine a very special favor. Hmmmm. And Alexandra Sellers is back in Desire with a fresh installment of her SONS OF THE DESERT series. *Sheikh's Castaway* will give you plenty of sweet (and naughty) dreams.

Even more shocking situations pop up in Linda Conrad's sensual *Between Strangers*. Imagine if you were stuck on the side of the road during a blizzard and a sexy cowboy offered *you* shelter from the storm…. (Hello, are you still with me?) Rounding out the month is Margaret Allison's *Principles and Pleasures*, a daring romp between a workaholic heroine and a man she doesn't know is actually her archenemy.

So settle in for some sensual, scandalous love stories…and enjoy every moment!

Melissa Jeglinski

Melissa Jeglinski
Senior Editor, Silhouette Desire

Please address questions and book requests to:
Silhouette Reader Service
U.S.: 3010 Walden Ave., P.O. Box 1325, Buffalo, NY 14269
Canadian: P.O. Box 609, Fort Erie, Ont. L2A 5X3

Sins of a Tanner

Peggy Moreland

Silhouette® Desire

Published by Silhouette Books

America's Publisher of Contemporary Romance

SILHOUETTE BOOKS

ISBN 0-373-76616-5

SINS OF A TANNER

Books by Peggy Moreland

Silhouette Desire

A Little Bit Country #515
Run for the Roses #598
Miss Prim #682
The Rescuer #765
Seven Year Itch #837
The Baby Doctor #867
Miss Lizzy's Legacy #921
A Willful Marriage #1024
Marry Me, Cowboy #1084
A Little Texas Two-Step #1090
Lone Star Kind of Man #1096
†*The Rancher's Spittin' Image* #1156
†*The Restless Virgin* #1163
†*A Sparkle in the Cowboy's Eyes* #1168
†*That McCloud Woman* #1227

Billionaire Bridegroom #1244
†*Hard Lovin' Man* #1270
‡*Ride a Wild Heart* #1306
‡*In Name Only* #1313
‡*Slow Waltz Across Texas* #1315
Groom of Fortune #1336
The Way to a Rancher's Heart #1345
Millionaire Boss #1365
The Texan's Tiny Secret #1394
Her Lone Star Protector #1426
**Five Brothers and a Baby* #1532
***Baby, You're Mine* #1544
***The Last Good Man in Texas* #1580
***Sins of a Tanner* #1616

Silhouette Special Edition

Rugrats and Rawhide #1084

Lone Star Country Club

An Arranged Marriage

*Trouble in Texas
†Texas Brides
‡Texas Grooms
**The Tanners of Texas

Silhouette Books

Turning Point 2002
"It Had To Be You"

Tanner's Millions

To the One I Love 2003
"Caught by a Cowboy"

PEGGY MORELAND

published her first romance with Silhouette in 1989 and continues to delight readers with stories set in her home state of Texas. Winner of the National Readers' Choice Award, a nominee for *Romantic Times* Reviewer's Choice Award and a two-time finalist for the prestigious RITA® Award, Peggy's books frequently appear on the *USA TODAY* and Waldenbooks bestseller lists. When not writing, you can usually find Peggy outside, tending the cattle, goats and other critters on the ranch she shares with her husband. You may write to Peggy at P.O. Box 1099, Florence, TX 76527-1099, or e-mail her at peggy@peggymoreland.com.

One

It was said that there wasn't a woman in the state of Texas who couldn't be seduced by a Tanner once he set his mind to the task. Tall in stature and richer than sin, with their coal-black hair and bedroom-blue eyes, the Tanner brothers were hard to resist.

Whit Tanner was the exception.

Though he stood over six feet tall and was easy enough on the eye, Whit looked nothing like the men whose name he shared. His hair was brown, not the expected black, and streaked with blond from years of working beneath a hot Texas sun. His eyes were brown, too, rather than the trademark blue, and almost the same color of his hair, thanks to the gold shot through the irises.

And the differences didn't stop there.

While it was a well-known fact the Tanner men

could charm the panties off a nun, the only females Whit felt comfortable around wore shoes shaped from iron and walked on four legs. When confronted with the human form of the gender, he tended to stammer and stutter and turn three shades of red—which might explain why he was still a bachelor at the ripe old age of twenty-nine.

Truth be known, Whit had never really thought much about his bachelor status one way or the other. He'd accepted his single state as just another curve life had thrown his way—or he had until all his step-brothers had started marrying and settling down.

First Ace had hitched himself to Maggie, then Woodrow had taken the fall with the doctor from Dallas. Ry had followed shortly thereafter when he'd hooked up with Kayla, the waitress from Austin who had stolen his heart. Together the two had stirred up a media blitz that had kept the Tanner name in the news for weeks. But it was when Rory, the confirmed bachelor of the bunch, had married Macy Keller that Whit had come to the slow realization that he was the last single Tanner.

"Last single Tanner," Whit muttered as he dragged the saddle down from the top rail of the round pen and swung it over the mare's back. He wasn't a Tanner. Not by birth, at any rate. He was the adopted son, the charity case Buck Tanner had taken on when he'd married Whit's mother.

Everybody in Tanner's Crossing, Whit included, had known that the marriage between Buck and Lee Grainger was no love match. A divorcée supporting herself and her young son on the tips she made waiting tables, Lee had been looking for security, while Buck had wanted someone to raise his four mother-less sons. In the deal they'd cut, Lee had gotten the home and security she'd desired and Buck had gotten himself a built-in maid and baby-sitter.

And Whit had gotten the Tanner name.

A rivulet of sweat coursed down between his eyes and dripped from the end of his nose. Shoving back his hat, he dragged a sleeve across his face. But looks and blood weren't all that distinguished him from the Tanners, he thought wearily as he settled his hat back over his head. Tanners didn't have to sweat out a living beneath a broiling sun.

Not unless they chose to, at any rate.

Puffing his cheeks, he blew out a breath, then reached beneath the horse for the cinch. But things could be worse, he told himself as he threaded the leather strap through the rigging ring. He could be stuck behind a desk in some office, shuffling papers, or trapped in some windowless factory putting to-gether widgits. Few men were able to work at a job they enjoyed...and Whit purely loved working with horses.

He supposed that was one thing he had Buck Tan-ner to thank for, as it was while working for Buck on the Bar-T, the Tanners's ranch, that Whit had discov-ered his affinity with horses. But that was all he'd thank Buck for, he thought bitterly. The man had made a lousy stepfather and, according to Whit's stepbrothers, a lousy father, as well.

He paused to frown. But was there such a thing as a *good* father?

He snorted a breath and fed another loop through the ring. How the hell would he know. His own had lit out just shy of his third birthday, leaving him and his mother to fend for themselves. He had thought the two of them were getting along just fine without a man around the house when one day, out of the blue, his mother had announced that she was marrying Buck and that he was going to adopt Whit. That Buck had agreed to adopt Whit had surprised some, as Buck had seldom had time for his own four sons. Whit soon learned he'd had even less for a stepson.

Scowling at the reminder of his stepfather's less than benevolent attitude toward him, he gave the cinch one last tug, making sure it was tight. The horse he was saddling—a green-broke sorrel mare—flattened her ears against her head and danced sideways at the increased pressure. He stroked a hand along the sorrel's neck.

"It's just a saddle, darlin'," he soothed. "I know it feels strange, but you'll get used to it in time."

Murmuring softly to the mare, he unfastened the lead rope he'd clipped to the halter and replaced it with a longe line, careful to keep his movements slow and easy so as not to spook the horse. Letting out some length in the rope, he smooched to the mare, encouraging her into a trot along the perimeter of the round pen. With the end of the rope gripped in one gloved hand, he turned a slow circle, keeping a steady eye on the mare's movements from his position in the center of the ring. After five nervous laps, the mare began to relax, gradually bringing her ears up and losing some of the prance in her gait.

He liked the looks of this little mare and hoped he could talk the owner into letting him train her for cutting. She'd make a good cutting horse. She was quick on the hoof, intelligent and responded well to commands. The true test would come when he put her nose-to-nose with a calf and saw how she handled herself under pressure.

The sound of a vehicle broke into his thoughts and he cocked his head slightly, listening to its approach. When the horse reached a spot along the fence that put him in line with the road, he glanced over the animal's back to see who was coming. A smile chipped at one corner of his mouth when he recognized his stepbrother Rory's truck. Riding shotgun was Macy, Rory's new wife.

While it was true that Whit despised Buck Tanner, his resentment didn't carry over to Buck's sons. He respected his stepbrothers, even liked them. Especially Rory. But he supposed that was because Rory was so damn easy to like.

"Hey, Whit!" Rory called as he and Macy climbed down from the truck. "Where'd you get that old nag?"

Whit chuckled as he maneuvered the horse to the center of the ring. "Better not let Dan Miller hear you call this mare a nag," he warned. "He paid a pretty penny for this little gal."

Rory opened the gate, held it while Macy stepped through, then followed her in. Macy made a beeline straight for Whit, her arms flung wide. He braced himself for the hug he knew was coming. Though he was growing rather used to all the female attention his sisters-in-law smothered him with, he still felt the familiar heat crawl up his neck as Macy wrapped her arms around him and squeezed.

He gave her an awkward one-armed hug in return. "Hey, Macy."

"Keep your hands to yourself," Rory complained, joining them. "That's my wife you're fondling."

"If this is your idea of fondling," Whit said wryly, "it's no wonder she latches on to me every time she sees me. The woman's desperate for affection."

"If she was, she wouldn't come to you lookin' for it," Rory replied, then hooted a laugh. "Hell, Whit. You wouldn't know what to do with a woman if one was hand-delivered to you with an instruction book attached."

Accustomed to Rory's teasing, Whit hid a smile as he led the horse to the fence and tethered it there. "Did y'all drive all the way out here to give me a hard time or is there a purpose for this visit?"

"We're here to deliver a personal invitation," Macy said. "The grand opening for my nursery is a week from this Saturday and I want you to come."

Whit turned, tugging off his gloves. "Grand opening, huh? Gonna have any good grub on hand?"

"Enough to feed a small army. I'm even serving champagne."

He winced at the mention of champagne. "This isn't going to be one of those fancy shindigs where I have to wear a suit, is it?"

Smiling, Macy gave his cheek an affectionate pat. "You can wear your birthday suit, for all I care."

"You expecting company?" Rory asked.

Whit glanced Rory's way, then followed his step-brother's gaze to the road and the approaching SUV.

Frowning, Whit shook his head. "Not that I'm aware of."

The three watched as the SUV came to a stop beside Rory's truck. Whit's gut clenched in denial when he recognized the woman behind the wheel.

"Isn't that Melissa Jacobs?" Rory asked curiously.

Whit quickly averted his gaze. "Yeah," he muttered as he jerked his gloves back on. "That's her, all right."

"Hey, Melissa," Rory called as the woman stepped from the vehicle. "Long time no see."

Lifting a hand in greeting, she crossed to join them in the pen. "It has been a while," she agreed as she accepted the hand Rory offered her. "It's good to see you, Rory."

"Good to see you, too." He tugged Macy forward. "I don't believe you've met my wife. Macy, Melissa Jacobs."

"Congratulations on your marriage," Melissa said as she shook Macy's hand, turning to include Rory in the well-wishes. "To you both."

"Thanks," Rory replied, then slowly sobered. "I sure was sorry to hear about Matt's death. Man, what a shock."

Her smile fading, she nodded. "Yes, it was."

"If there's anything I can do…"

"No," she said quickly, "but I appreciate the thought."

"So," Rory said in an obvious effort to change the subject, "what brings you all the way out here?"

"I came to see Whit."

Rory caught Macy's elbow. "Then we'll get out of your way."

Whit had remained silent and watchful throughout the exchange, but panicked at the thought of being left alone with Melissa. "There's no need for y'all to run off," he said in a rush. "As soon as I'm done here, we can go up to the house and get us something cool to drink."

Rory glanced at his watch, then shook his head. "Sorry, bro, but we'll have to take a rain check. We left Macy's dad at the nursery alone, and he's liable to disown us if a shipment of plants arrives and he has to unload the truck by himself. See you Sunday at lunch," he called as he herded Macy toward the truck.

"I hope they didn't leave on my account."

Whit glanced Melissa's way, then away, with a frown. "You heard what he said. They had to get back to the nursery." Keeping his back to her, he lifted a stirrup and hooked it over the saddle horn. "Matt's been dead, what? Four months now? Shouldn't you be home grieving?"

He heard her shocked intake of breath and knew that what he'd said was uncalled for. Even cruel. But he didn't care. An eye for an eye. Isn't that what the Good Book taught? You hurt me, I hurt you back.

"I didn't come here to be insulted," she said tersely.

"Then why are you here?"

"I have a horse I want you to break."

He continued to unsaddle the mare, keeping his

gaze fixed on the task and his back to her. "There are other trainers available. If you don't know one, I can give you a name."

"I don't want just any trainer. The horse…is Matt's."

Her hesitancy in identifying the horse's owner was obvious…and telling. Matt Jacobs. Melissa's husband and Whit's best friend.

Ex-best friend, he thought bitterly.

His scowl deepening, he dragged off the saddle and swung it up to balance on the top rail. He knew the horse she wanted him to break. Matt had purchased the stud as a colt several years back, with the intent to train him for the racetrack. The horse's bloodlines were impressive. Unfortunately his temperament wasn't.

Grabbing a brush, he swept it across the mare's back in short, impatient strokes. "Why not just sell the damn horse?" he said irritably. "He'd bring a fair price."

"He'll bring a better one if he's trained."

He heard the determination in her voice and a hint of something more. *Desperation?*

Refusing to be moved by it, he shook his head and continued to brush down the horse. "I've got a list a mile long of people waiting for me to train their horses. I haven't got time to take on any more."

"I'll pay you your standard fee, plus a percentage of the horse's sale price."

Startled by the unusual offer, he glanced her way…and immediately wished he hadn't. Seeing her again brought every memory, every heartbreak, winging back. Eyes the color of aged whiskey; long, honey-blond hair that tumbled over her shoulders in soft waves; delicate features that had haunted his nights for seven long years.

Tearing his gaze away, he tossed the brush into the tack box and plucked out a currycomb. "Like I said. I don't need any more business."

"Whit, please—"

"No," he snapped, then spun to glare at her. "Now, if you want me to recommend someone, I will. Otherwise I'd appreciate it if you'd get off my land."

Melissa sat parked in front of the school, her SUV at the head of the car pool line. A soft breeze blew through the open window on her left, ruffling her hair, but it didn't come close to cooling the heat in her cheeks. She was embarrassed. Humiliated. Furious. Panic-stricken. It had taken her weeks to work up the nerve to approach Whit about breaking Matt's horse. Weeks spent searching for another option, anything, so long as it didn't include Whit. In the end, she was forced to admit he was her only option.

And he'd turned her down flat.

Not that she had expected him to leap at her offer. She'd known going in that there was a strong chance he would refuse. What she hadn't known was how much it would hurt when he did.

The doors to the school flew open and children spilled out, shrieking and laughing as they raced for the cars that lined the narrow lane. Melissa quickly unfastened her seat belt and pushed open her door.

Before she could step down, a pair of arms vised around her legs.

"Hi, Mom!"

Chuckling, she scrubbed her knuckles over her son's blond hair. "Hi, yourself, kiddo." She reached down and lifted him up and over her, then plopped him into the passenger seat beside her.

"And how was your day?" she asked as she fastened the seat belt around him.

"Joey Matthews threw up all over his art paper and Shane Ragsdale's dog had thirteen puppies. Can I have one? Please? Can I?"

She turned the key, starting the engine. "We already have a dog," she reminded him.

"Yeah, but Champ's not mine. He's yours. I want a puppy that's all mine."

She checked for traffic, then pulled out onto the street. "One dog is all we can handle right now."

"*Please*, Mom?" he begged, straining against the seat belt. "I'll feed him and take care of him. You won't have to do nothin', I promise."

"Anything," she corrected automatically, then sighed, feeling as if she was always saying no to her son. "We can't afford to feed another animal right now," she explained gently. "You know that."

He slumped against the seat in a sulk. "Being poor sucks," he mumbled.

"Grady Jacobs!" she cried. "We are *not* poor."

"Then how come you have to sell Dad's horse?"

"Because we need money more than we need a horse," she replied, then gave him a stern look. "But that does *not* mean we are poor.'' Jutting her chin, she faced the windshield again. ''We're just experiencing a temporary cash flow problem.''

''Angela Hanes's mom said we don't have a pot to pee in or a window to throw it out.''

It was all she could do to keep the vehicle on the road. ''Angela's mother said that to you?'' she asked in amazement.

''No, Angela did. She heard her mom talking to Mrs. Henley on the phone. I asked Angela what it meant and she said it meant we're poor. That when Dad died he left us broke.''

She narrowed her eyes, furious to know that her friends and neighbors were talking about her behind her back. ''Well, Mrs. Hanes is wrong,'' she informed him. ''We are *not* broke.''

''Then why can't I have a puppy?''

She closed her eyes a moment, praying for patience, for just the right words to make her son understand their financial situation without letting him know how desperate it really was.

''Before Matt died,'' she said carefully, ''we had two incomes to pay our bills. With him gone now, we only have the money I make.''

''I could help you so you could earn more money.''

Her heart melting at the offer, she reached to smooth the hair back from his brow. ''Thanks, sweetheart. But I don't want you worrying about our financial situation, okay? Once we sell Matt's horse, everything will be fine.''

And everything would be fine, she told herself as she turned her gaze to the road again.

Just as soon as she found someone to break Matt's horse.

After the unexpected visit from Melissa on Monday, Whit's week went downhill in a hurry. Tuesday, one of the studs in his care cut his foreleg while fighting with another stud through the fence that separated them. It required a call to the vet and another to inform the stud's owner, which cost him almost a full day's work. To make matters worse, Wednesday night a raccoon got into the feed room and tore into the sacks of oats stored there, ruining three perfectly good sacks of feed and creating a hell of a mess for Whit to clean up on Thursday. Then on Sunday, a gelding Whit was working with bucked him off, conveniently dumping him in a fresh pile of manure. By the time he returned the horse to its stall and limped back to the house for a shower and a change of clothes, it was pushing noon.

He considered blowing off going to the Bar-T, where his stepbrothers and their families gathered for Sunday lunch, and kicking back with a beer and an afternoon of ESPN instead. But he knew, if he did, the entire Tanner clan would probably show up at his house, looking for him.

Shuddering at the thought of having all those people crammed into his small house, he climbed into his truck and made the drive to the Bar-T. Thanks to the gelding and the landing spot he'd chosen for Whit, he was the last to arrive.

"Sorry I'm late," he said as he slid into the empty chair beside Rory.

Rory glanced his way, then pulled back, with a frown. "What happened to you?"

Grimacing, Whit rubbed a self-conscious hand over the bruise the fall had left on his cheek. "Horse pitched me off."

Ry passed Whit a platter stacked high with chicken-fried steak. "If you want, I can take a look at that for you later," he offered. "Make sure there aren't any broken bones."

Whit forked up a steak and dropped it onto his plate before passing the platter on. "It's nothing. Just a bruise."

Maggie gave her husband, Ace, a pointed look. "I've heard that one before," she said dryly.

Familiar with the story of Ace's fall from a horse and his refusal to allow Maggie to take him to the doctor, everyone shared a laugh at Ace's expense.

"Laugh all you want," Ace said grumpily. "But a man who can't take a tumble from a horse, without running to some sawbones to get patched up, isn't much of a man. Right, Whit?"

Whit glanced around the table. With two doctors and two nurses waiting expectantly for his answer, he decided discretion was the better part of valor. "Whatever you say, Ace."

"Coward," Rory said out of the corner of his mouth.

"I've already got one bruise," Whit told him. "I'm not looking for another."

With a rueful shake of his head, Rory returned to his meal.

"Looks like the lawyers are going to have the old

man's estate ready to settle in a couple of weeks,''
Ace said. "We'll need to pick a time we can all meet
to sign the necessary papers.''

A discussion followed, but Whit tuned it out and
focused on his meal. Although Ace had told him he
would inherit a fifth of the old man's estate, the same
as the rest of his stepbrothers, Whit had informed Ace
that he wanted no part of anything that was Buck's.

"What about you, Whit?'' Ace asked. "Is May 29
at two all right with you?''

Caught with his fork halfway to his mouth, Whit
glanced around the table and found everyone looking
at him expectantly. He slowly lowered the fork to his
plate. "I already told y'all I don't want any part of
Buck's estate.''

"And we understand your reasons for feeling that
way,'' Ace assured him. "But you're getting an equal
share the same as the rest of us, whether you want it
or not.''

"You know damned good and well that if Buck
had left a will, he wouldn't have named me in it,''
Whit said.

"That may be true,'' Ace conceded. "But there's
a strong chance he wouldn't have named us, either,
since he wasn't on speaking terms with any of his
offspring at the time of his death. Since he didn't
leave a will, the law requires that his estate be divided
equally among his children.''

"I'm not one of his children,'' Whit reminded him.

"By law you are. I have the adoption papers to
prove it.''

Whit slumped back in his chair. "Come on, Ace,''

he said in frustration. "Can't you just tell the lawyers to cut me out?"

Ace opened his hands in a helpless gesture. "Sorry, the law is the law. And without your signature," he added, "the estate can't be settled, nor can the assets be awarded." Knowing he'd put Whit on the spot, he reared back smugly in his chair. "So, how does May 29 at two work for you to meet and sign the papers?"

Scowling, Whit stabbed his fork into his steak. "I'll sign whatever papers are necessary, but I'll never touch a cent of Buck's money."

"That's your prerogative," Rory said, then quickly changed the subject. "So what was Melissa doing over at your house the other day?"

His frown deepening, Whit cut into his steak. "She wanted me to break a horse for her."

"Melissa Jacobs?" Elizabeth, Woodrow's wife, asked curiously.

"One and the same," Rory replied, then gave Whit a speculative look. "Didn't the two of you use to date?"

Whit stiffened, unaware that Rory—or anyone else, for that matter—had known that he'd dated Melissa. Breaking open a roll, he lifted his shoulder in what he hoped came across as an indifferent shrug. "We went out for a while."

"Really?" Ace said. "I didn't know Melissa ever dated anyone other than Matt."

And you could've gone on thinking that, Whit thought resentfully, *if Rory had kept his dang mouth shut.*

Avoiding Ace's gaze, he slathered his roll with butter. "Like I said, it was only for a while."

Elizabeth shook her head sadly. "I don't know Melissa all that well, but I feel so sorry for her. Losing a husband in such a tragic accident is bad enough, but to discover that he has left you penniless must be awful."

Whit slowly lowered his knife to his plate and stared at Elizabeth. "Matt left Melissa broke?"

Elizabeth glanced uneasily at the others at the table. "Well, yes. At least, that's what I heard. I assumed it was true."

"It's true enough," Woodrow confirmed. "Dillon Phillips bought a plow from her last week. Said he got it for a good price as she needed the money to make her mortgage."

Whit snorted a breath and picked up his fork. "If that's the story she gave him, she was feeding him a line of bull. There's no mortgage on that property. I know for a fact that Matt inherited the farm free and clear from his granddaddy." He scooped up a forkful of potatoes, then added, "But even if it was true she was broke, Melissa wouldn't have to sell off assets to make her note. Mike would give her whatever she needed."

Macy held up a hand. "Wait a minute. You've lost me. Who is Mike and what does he have to do with Melissa?"

"Mike's Melissa's father," Rory explained. "Lives over in Lampasas. He and Buck were old running buddies. With Buck gone now, Mike's probably the single most wealthy man around these parts."

"If that's the case," Macy said, "then it would seem that she'd ask her father for money, if she truly needed it."

"Not necessarily."

When everyone turned to look at Kayla, she lifted her hands. "Heck, I wouldn't. It's a matter of pride."

Ry gave his wife's arm an indulgent pat. "Yes, dear. We're all familiar with your pride."

"Kayla may have a point," Rory said in his sister-in-law's defense. "If you think about it, it's the only explanation that makes any sense. As I recall, Melissa and Mike butted heads a lot while she was growing up."

"I can vouch for that," Ace agreed. "I remember more than once hearing Mike complain to Buck about Melissa being stubborn as a mule."

"Then it's unlikely that she would go to her father for help," Elizabeth said, then shook her head sadly. "And that makes me feel even more sorry for her. At a time like this, a woman needs the support of her family."

Whit swallowed hard. He knew from personal experience that Rory's and Ace's comments about Mike and Melissa butting heads were true. Mike was a hard man to get along with under any circumstances, but the level of control he'd tried to wield over his only daughter would have made even the most docile of individuals fight at the chains he kept her bound with.

And Elizabeth was right, as well. Considering Melissa's past relationship with her father, it seemed unlikely that she would turn to him in her time of need.

But if she couldn't go to her father for help, he wondered, who could she go to?

He wiped a shaky hand down his mouth, remembering her visit to his place and the desperation in her voice, when she'd asked him to train the horse.

And how had he responded to her plea for help?

He'd not only refused, he'd ordered her off his land.

He quickly shook off the guilt that tried to settle on his shoulders. He wouldn't feel badly about the way he'd treated Melissa. Hell, why should he? he thought defensively. She'd certainly never concerned herself with his feelings. He'd given her his heart and what had she done in return?

She'd eloped with his best friend.

Two

Though Whit continued to fight the guilt, it dogged his steps for a week, distracting him from his work and robbing him of much-needed sleep at night. He didn't want to feel badly for the way he'd treated Melissa. And he sure as hell didn't want to feel sorry for her. But that's exactly what he found himself doing throughout the week.

By Saturday he was willing to do just about anything to shake loose from the guilt, and the grand opening for Nature's Way, Macy's landscape and nursery business, offered him the perfect escape. He wasn't much on socializing, but he figured going to the grand opening was better than spending another evening at home alone with his conscience.

Even if he did have to wear a suit.

In spite of his anxiousness to attend the party, he

was one of the last to arrive and had to park two blocks away and walk to the greenhouse where the opening was to take place.

One step inside the cavernous building reminded him why he normally avoided social gatherings. The noise level alone would have made a deaf man clap his hands over his ears. The music itself wasn't too bad—or at least what he could hear of it sounded pleasant enough. It was the hundred or so conversations going on at the same time that made his head ache.

A waiter rushed by, balancing a tray filled with flutes of champagne on his shoulder, and Whit quickly stepped out of the way to avoid a collision. Easing back to stand against the wall and out of harm's way, he stuffed his hands into his pockets and looked around.

The last time he'd visited the nursery, the greenhouse had looked like…well, a greenhouse, with long wooden tables laden with plants running the length of the room and tangled hoses trailing over the floor. Now the place looked more like one of those fancy solariums he'd seen featured in the home and garden magazines his sisters-in-law were always drooling over—a fete he figured only Macy could pull off with such style.

A huge tree-shaped fountain, carved from native limestone, rose from the center of a grouping of curved buffet tables. Water bubbled up from the tree's dome and flowed down over intricately carved leaves to tumble into a shallow pool below. Rimmed with vases of fresh-cut flowers that scented the air and strategically placed lighting, the pool and fountain created a spectacular centerpiece for the mouthwatering feast of hors d'oeuvres placed around it.

Above him, miniature lights had been strung along the steel beams that formed the glass roof, giving the ceiling the appearance of a star-filled sky. Urns and pots filled with lush tropical plants occupied every available nook, while tall Norfolk pines stood like sentinels at each of the three doorways. Along the outer walls of the building hung baskets filled with an assortment of flowers and vines, adding yet another splash of color and texture to the space.

Though impressed with Macy's decorating skills, to truly enjoy it, Whit would have needed a hammock and about two hours alone. For a man who spent the majority of his time in the country, conducting one-sided conversations with horses, the press of people and the noise they created were almost more than he could bear.

Deciding that an evening at home with his conscience didn't seem so bad after all, he began to ease his way down the wall, craning his neck as he searched for Macy, so he could make an appearance and split. Just as he spotted her, his hip bumped something solid and he made a wild grab to keep the object from falling.

"Hey!" Macy cried. "Careful with the merchandise."

His smile sheepish, he righted what appeared to be an old garden gate. "Sorry, Mace," he said, then glanced down at his hands and the rust that covered them. "Uh, you might want to have a talk with your supplier. Looks like he's selling you inferior products."

"Are you kidding me? Salvaged iron is the rage! This stuff flies out of the store faster than I can slap a price tag on it."

Giving her a skeptical look, Whit squatted in front of the gate to examine it more closely. Though old and no longer functional, someone had given it new life by attaching glass jars to the scrolled iron that formed it. Secured by a fine-gauge wire, the jars held lighted votive candles and fresh-cut flowers.

Impressed by the ingenious use of material, Whit pushed his hands against his knees and stood. "Okay," he conceded. "I have to admit that's pretty darn clever."

She lifted a brow. "It can be yours for a price."

He sputtered a laugh. "And what would I do with a piece of foolishness like that?"

"Oh, I don't know," she said, hiding a smile. "I suppose you could set it up on your patio and wow the ladies you entertain at home."

"What ladies?" he asked wryly.

"My point exactly," she said as she looped her arm through his and led him toward the crowd. "You need to get out more. Go places where you can meet single women your age."

"Aw, Macy," he complained. "Don't start with me. You know how I am around women. Especially ones I don't know."

"Fine. Then we'll find a woman you *do* know for you to talk to."

He tugged her to a stop and lifted a brow. "I am. I'm talking to you."

"A *single* woman," she clarified.

He did a quick scan of the crowd, then shrugged. "Sorry, but it appears all the women here are either married or engaged."

Macy snagged the arm of a woman who was passing by. "This one's not."

"Whoa," the woman said, laughing as Macy hauled her back. "What am I not?"

"Married," Macy replied. "Whit was complaining that every woman here was either married or engaged. I just proved him wrong."

As the woman turned to look at Whit, resentment knotted in his gut when he discovered that out of all the available women in the room, Macy had chosen Melissa Jacobs to prove her point.

"I should have added widow to that list," he muttered, then turned on his heel and walked away.

The next morning Whit was in the barn early, cleaning out the stalls. It was a hot, backbreaking job, but it suited his mood just fine as he had some steam to work off.

He couldn't believe he'd run into Melissa the night before. The odds of seeing her twice in a two-week span, after successfully avoiding her for nearly seven years, had to be high.

But Whit's luck had never been very good. Not where Melissa was concerned.

"I think you owe me an explanation."

Startled by the voice, he snapped up his head to

find Macy standing in the stall's open doorway. That she was angry with him was obvious in the hands she held fisted against her hips.

With a frown, he resumed his shoveling. "For what?"

Dropping her hands, she marched toward him. "Don't you play dumb with me, Whit Tanner. You know very well that you were rude to Melissa last night, and I want to know why."

"No offense, Macy, but you're not my mother."

"A fact you should be grateful for," she informed him. "If I was, I'd turn you over my knee and give you a spanking you wouldn't soon forget."

He snorted a breath. "I'd like to see you try."

"Don't tempt me," she warned. "I'm about a hair away from snatching you bald-headed as it is."

He stood the shovel up and braced an arm over the handle to peer at her. "Do you talk to Rory like that?"

"Don't try to change the subject. I want an explanation, and I'm not leaving until I get one."

To prove her point, she sat on a bale of hay and folded her arms across her chest. The clencher for Whit, though, was when she pursed her lips and lifted an expectant brow.

Grimacing, he shot the shovel blade beneath a pile of manure and scooped it up, planning to ignore her. He crossed to the wheelbarrow, dumped the manure, then repeated the process four more times. By the time he shot the shovel beneath the fifth pile, her steady gaze was burning a hole in his back and the heavy silence that stretched between them was screaming in his ears.

"Okay!" he said in frustration. "I left because I didn't want to talk to her."

"Why not?"

"Because I *didn't*. Period." He scooped up manure, then turned to frown at her. "And you might as well go on home and irritate Rory for a while, because that's the only explanation you're going to get from me."

Jutting her chin, she stood. "All right. I'll go. But not before I have my say. Last night you insulted not only one of my guests, but one of my suppliers as well, and I think you owe her an apology."

"If by supplier you mean Melissa, you're crazy as a loon. She's never worked a day in her life."

"That just proves how little you know. I've bought a number of her creations, including the garden gate you tripped over."

When he merely looked at her, she sagged her shoulders in frustration. "I know you're shy around women, Whit. But you're not a mean person. In fact, I can't think of another man with a heart as soft as yours. That's why it's so hard for me to understand why you'd intentionally hurt a woman who has suffered such a tremendous loss, one who is struggling so hard to pull herself out of debt."

"I did nothing but walk away. If that offended her, that's her problem, not mine."

"Her husband was your friend," she reminded him stubbornly. "And from what Rory has told me, your *best* friend. If for no other reason than out of respect for Matt, I would think you could put aside whatever differences you might have with his wife, and offer her the kindness and support she needs and deserves."

Macy may not have gotten the explanation or apology she thought she deserved from Whit, but she had succeeded in making him feel like a heel, a trait he didn't feel he deserved.

Yeah, you do, his conscience argued. *Macy was right. Matt was your friend. Your* best *friend. And friends take care of friends.*

Scowling, Whit lifted a bale of hay high and heaved it onto the growing stack in the barn's loft. "Matt was a friend, all right," he muttered as he reached for another bale. "The minute I turned my back, he stole my girl."

Your girl?

Yes, dammit, Whit thought angrily as he hefted the bale up. She might have been Matt's girl first, but she'd broken things off with him and started dating Whit. And she'd still be Whit's girl now, maybe even his wife, if Matt hadn't stolen her away.

What did he do? Hold a gun to her head? Hog-tie and gag her? Surely, Matt isn't the only one to blame.

His scowl deepening, Whit shoved the bale onto the stack. No, Melissa owned a part, as well. She'd made Whit fall in love with her. Even claimed to love him, too. Then, the minute he'd left town, she'd run off with his best friend.

There. You admitted it. Matt was your best friend. Y'all sure had some good times together. Remember

*the night the two of you stole a six-pack of beer out
of Matt's parents' refrigerator and got drunk as
skunks out by the lake?*

Grimacing, Whit tugged off his work gloves. Yeah,
he remembered that night, all right. And others, as
well.

With a sigh, he sank onto a bale of hay and dropped
his forehead to his hands, unable to stop the memories
from surfacing.

Growing up, he and Matt had all but lived together,
spending almost every waking hour in each other's
company. Before his mother had married Buck and
was still working at the café in town, she had arranged
for Whit to go home with Matt after school each day.
He and Matt would play some ball, watch a little television, wrestle on the floor. His first black eye was
courtesy of a left Matt had thrown that Whit hadn't
dodged in time.

Even after his mother and Buck had married and
Whit had moved to Buck's ranch, he and Matt had
managed to continue their friendship. Matt was the
one who had listened to all of Whit's frustrations of
living in the Tanner household. And it was Matt who
had helped him devise the scheme the time he'd
planned to run away.

And it was Matt who was the first to appear at the
Tanner's door the day Whit's mother was killed in a
car wreck.

He gulped back emotion as an image of Matt as
he'd looked that day formed in his mind—standing
on the porch, his hat in his hands, tears streaming
down his face. Whit had needed Matt that day.

Needed the comfort and strength his friend had offered as he'd faced the biggest tragedy of his life.

And he'd needed his friend in the days that had followed, when Whit had announced to Buck that he was moving out and Buck had refused to let him go. Since Buck had adopted Whit, by law he was Whit's legal guardian. And there was no way Buck was going to let Whit leave when he represented a source of free labor for the Tanner ranch.

Matt had stood by Whit, with him, helping to make the intolerable tolerable. Without his friend, Whit wasn't sure he would've survived those last few years he'd lived under Buck's dominating rule.

Guilt tried to settle itself on his shoulders again, but he stubbornly shook it off. He wouldn't feel badly for not helping Matt's widow. He didn't believe for a minute that Matt had left Melissa in the dire financial straits his family insisted she was in. Hell! Matt wasn't an extravagant man. He might have come from money, but he was a good ol' country boy with simple taste and simpler needs, same as Whit.

At least that was the kind of man Matt had been when he and Whit were still running around together. Had he changed that much over the years?

Whit dropped his hands to his thighs with a sigh of defeat. It didn't matter if Matt had changed or not, he told himself as he pushed to his feet. Matt had been a friend, a good friend. And just as his conscience had reminded him, friends took care of friends.

Or, in this case, a friend's family.

* * *

Melissa laced her fingers together to keep from wringing her hands as she trailed the trainer, watching as he threw his gear into the back of his truck. He was the third man she'd hired for the job in the same number of days and the third one to leave without so much as laying a hand on the horse.

"I know War Lord can be difficult," she began uneasily.

"*Difficult?*" he repeated, then barked a laugh and climbed into his truck. "Lady, that horse isn't *difficult*. He's plumb crazy!"

"Please," she begged. "Give him another chance. I'm sure he'll settle down once he gets used to you."

Heaving a sigh, the man braced his arm on the open window frame and leaned out. "Look, lady," he said kindly. "That horse is never gonna amount to anything. You can't even sell him for glue, what with him refusing to load into a trailer. If you want, I'll put him down for you. No charge."

Sickened by the suggestion, she stepped back, shaking her head. "N-no. I won't put him down. I can't."

With a shrug, he pulled his arm inside. "It's your nightmare."

She watched him drive away, sure that he was taking with him her last hope of paying off her debts. She'd already contacted every trainer within a hundred-mile radius. There was no one left for her to call. It was all she could do to keep from sinking to the ground and crying like a baby.

But crying wouldn't solve her problems. She'd

shed enough tears over the past four months to know
that crying wouldn't get her out of the mess Matt had
left her in. Aware of that, she squared her shoulders
and turned for the house and the studio behind it.

Throughout her marriage to Matt, the studio had
served as a refuge for her as well as a place for her
to work. Today, more than ever, she needed the solace
it offered. As she stepped inside, walls painted a soft,
soothing blue seemed to wrap themselves around her
and pull her in. Everything in the room, from the
braided rag rug on the floor to the ceiling fan that
stirred the air, she'd chosen herself. More, she'd purchased them with money she'd earned with her own
two hands. And it was that feeling of independence,
that sense of accomplishment, that carried her on to
the worktable that stood on the far side of the room.

Stopping in front of the table, she ran a hand lightly
over the edge of the half-finished frame she'd been
working on prior to the trainer telling her he was quit-
ting. The tiles of broken china that covered half the
frame's face were cool to the touch and rough with
dried grout. A pile of unused tiles lay near at hand,
waiting to be fitted into place.

Here was the familiar, she thought as she slid onto
the stool. The sure. Everything else in her life might
be in chaos, but in this one room was peace. Here she
was in control.

With her mind already focusing in on the design,
she selected a tile and set to work.

Whit gazed at the Lone Star flag painted on the
roof of the horse barn as he drove past, wondering if

Matt had painted the design himself or hired it done. In either case, he liked the tribute to their home state of Texas and wouldn't mind having a similar one painted on the roof of his own barn.

Focusing his gaze back on the road, he drove the remaining distance to the house, turned off the engine, then sank back and simply stared, remembering the first time Matt had brought him to the house. Matt had been higher than a kite that day, excited about the prospect of living on his own for the first time.

But living on his own was all Matt had to be excited about, he thought wryly as the house hadn't amounted to much back then. An inheritance from his granddaddy, the house had stood vacant for nearly a year before Matt had taken possession of it. Judging by its condition at the time, it had been neglected for a good deal longer than that. Grass had stood knee-high in the yard and loose panels of tin on the roof had flapped in the afternoon breeze, creating an eery sound. But as Matt had said when Whit had commented on the house's poor condition, "Hell, it's free! Who can complain about that?"

Whit certainly couldn't…and hadn't. At the time he'd still been living at the Bar-T under Buck's rule and would've given his right arm to have a place to call his own, even if that place was in danger of collapse at any given moment.

But the house Whit sat in front of now held little resemblance to the one Matt had shown him that day. Fresh paint and a new roof had gone a long way toward improving its appearance. But there was another quality that increased its appeal. Something that could only be sensed, not seen.

Somewhere along the way, the house had become a home.

He could all but feel the warmth that emanated from it, smell the scent of fresh-baked bread wafting from the open windows. A swing suspended from the ceiling of the covered front porch swung lazily in the afternoon breeze, the pillows scattered along its back plump and inviting. Clay pots filled with bright geraniums edged the steps, while tall wicker planters holding lacy-leafed ferns welcomed guests from either side of the door.

He wanted to believe that Matt was responsible for the changes, just as he wanted to believe that Matt had painted the Lone Star flag on the barn roof. But he knew better. Matt was never one to fret much over appearances. He was just too darn lazy to put forth the effort. If left up to him, the house—as well as the barn—would have remained in the same condition as the day he had moved in.

That left only one person who could be responsible for the changes.

Melissa.

Which made Whit wonder if she was also the one responsible for the debts Matt had supposedly left behind. It wasn't a stretch to imagine her requesting— maybe even demanding—that he remodel the house. More so than Matt, she had come from money and was used to having the best of everything. Her father's home in Lampasas was nothing short of a mansion, complete with a live-in housekeeper, cook and

full-time groundskeeper. For her to leave all that op-
ulence and move into Matt's house must have been a
shock for her.

But from the looks of things, she hadn't wasted any
time bringing the house up to her standards.

Setting his jaw against the resentment that rose, he
climbed down from his truck and strode to the front
door, anxious to get his business with her over with
and be on his way. He rapped his knuckles hard
against the screen door, then waited. When no sound
came from within, he glanced around, then headed
for the rear of the house. A shed at the back of the
yard caught his attention and made him stop and stare.
He remembered the building from his first visit to
Matt's place as looking as if it was one strong wind
away from collapse. Nothing at all like it appeared
now.

The wood frame structure had been painted a soft,
buttery yellow and trimmed out in a crisp, clean
white. The glass in the two windows that faced the
front gleamed in the afternoon sunshine and reflected
images of the flowers that spilled from the window
boxes suspended below them. Though the afternoon
was hot, a Dutch-style door was propped open to
catch the occasional breeze.

Drawn by the open doorway, curious, Whit crossed
the yard to peer inside. Against the far wall, he found
Melissa sitting with her back to him, her head bent
over some unseen task. Since she didn't appear to
have heard his approach, he took a moment to look
around.

The room was crowded with a wild assortment of

items yet he sensed an order to the chaos. Shelving lined the two longest walls and held buckets of paint, tools and what looked to be jars filled with beads and buttons. A child's playpen was angled into a far corner and stacked high with old, faded quilts. To his left, salvaged iron was propped against the wall, visual proof that Melissa had designed the gate he had tripped over at the grand opening, just as Macy had claimed.

Not liking the stab of guilt that accompanied the discovery, he scowled.

"Where do you get all this junk?"

Startled, Melissa spun on the stool, her eyes wide in alarm. They narrowed to slits when her gaze met his.

Snatching a rag from the table behind her, she stood and wiped her fingers with quick, angry jerks of her hand. "If you've come to insult me again, you can leave."

He was tempted to do just that. Leave. She was the one who needed him. He sure as hell didn't need her *or* her attitude.

But he'd come to help out a friend, he reminded himself. And he wasn't leaving until he had.

Dragging off his hat, he stepped inside.

"I stopped by to take a look at that horse you wanted me to train."

She eyed him suspiciously. "I thought you said you didn't have time to take on any more clients."

He lifted a shoulder. "Seems now I do."

She eyed him a moment longer, then turned her back and swiped the rag over the tabletop, sending white dust to clog the air. "Sorry. But I've already hired someone else."

He knew she was lying and knew how to prove it, too. "Who?"

She froze, her fingers knotting in the rag. Forcing her hand into motion again, she said, "That's none of your business."

"I'm making it mine."

When she didn't respond, he lost what little patience he had left with her. Crossing the room in two long strides, he grabbed her elbow and spun her around to face him.

"Listen, dammit," he said angrily. "I know you're in a bind and I'm here to offer my help."

Though the grip he had on her was strong, she didn't cower in fear, as he might have expected. Instead she met his gaze squarely and with an anger that matched his own.

"Why would you want to help me?"

He released her arm with a force that sent her stumbling back a step. "Don't kid yourself, Melissa. I wouldn't spit on you, if you were on fire. I'm doing this for Matt. He was my friend."

"Friend?" she repeated incredulously. "How can you claim to be his friend when you couldn't even be bothered to come to his funeral?"

Shame burned through Whit, but he refused to let her see it. No, he hadn't gone to Matt's funeral. But it wasn't because he hadn't wanted to be there. He'd wanted to go, if for no other reason than to honor the friendship the two had once shared. But he'd deliberately stayed away, knowing that, if he went, he'd see Melissa.

But he wouldn't tell her that. If he did, she might think he still had feelings for her. And he felt nothing for her. Nothing at all.

"Matt *was* my friend," he maintained stubbornly. "And he'd still be my friend today if you hadn't come between us."

She paled at the accusation, then quickly turned away.

But not before Whit saw the guilt that stained her cheeks.

She inhaled a deep breath, then turned to face him, her chin tilted high enough to catch water. "All right. If training the horse will clear your conscience, then you have my permission to train it."

Clear his conscience? he thought in amazement. It wasn't *his* conscience that needed clearing. But she could believe whatever she wanted to believe. He'd come to do a favor for an old friend, not to get into a spitting contest with that friend's widow.

Ramming his hat over his head, he turned for the door. "I'll load him up and take him to my place."

"You can't."

He stopped, barely able to contain his frustration. "You just said I could train him."

"He doesn't load."

Praying he'd misunderstood, he turned to look at her. "The horse doesn't load?"

She shook her head.

He was tempted to tell her to forget it, that he didn't have time to drive the sixty-plus miles to

Briggs and back every day that working with the horse would require. But he'd come to return a favor to a friend and he wasn't going to back out now just because of a little inconvenience.

Dragging off his hat, he pushed his fingers through his hair. "That's gonna change things some," he said as he worked through his schedule in his mind. "I have stock to feed at my own place, plus a few that'll require exercise before I can head this way. I probably wouldn't be able to make it over here until noon or so."

Judging by the way she pursed her lips, he assumed she wasn't too pleased with the time he'd named. But what difference did it make if he came at sunup or sundown? he asked himself. Either way, the horse got trained, and that was what she wanted, wasn't it?

Already questioning his sanity in making the offer, he snugged on his hat and turned to leave again. "Look for me around noon tomorrow."

Melissa didn't want to *look* for Whit, at all. If she never laid eyes on him again, she would die a happy woman.

But looking for him was exactly what she found herself doing the next day as the clock slowly wound its way to noon.

He finally showed up at nine minutes after twelve. She knew the exact moment of his arrival because she glanced at the wall clock above her worktable when she heard his truck, and quickly did the math to see how much time remained before she had to pick up Grady from school. Two hours. Would that give Whit enough time to work with the horse and be gone before she returned?

Intending to ask him how long he planned to stay, she turned to look out the window again and was surprised to see that he had turned onto the lane that led to the barn instead of continuing on to the house.

Irritated that he didn't think it necessary to check in with her before beginning work, she pursed her lips and turned her attention back to the cutter quilt she had spread over her worktable and the pattern pinned to it. Well, she certainly wasn't going to make the long trek to the barn to see if he needed anything, she told herself as she pushed a tracing wheel along the pattern. Not in this heat. If he had any questions, he could darn well come to her. She was the one paying him, after all. Not the other way around.

Reminded of the money she would owe him, she caught her lower lip between her teeth. She didn't have the money to pay Whit. Not and pay her monthly bills, too.

She blew out a breath. "Who am I trying to kid?" she muttered as she pressed the wheel against the quilt again. She wouldn't have the money to pay him even if she *didn't* pay her bills.

But he'd get what was due him, she told herself. She'd see that he did. He just wouldn't get it until he'd completed the job and the horse was sold. She'd done her research. At the price War Lord would bring, she'd have enough money to pay Whit his trainer's fee, plus the percentage of the sale price she had promised him, and still have enough left to pay off a large portion of Matt's debts.

She cast an uneasy glance over her shoulder. Or she would if Whit was able to train the horse. The other three men she'd hired for the job had been unable to get close enough to the horse to touch him, much less work with him.

Reminded of the horse's mean disposition, she caught her lower lip between her teeth again and worried it as she strained to see the area surrounding the barn. She really should at least warn Whit that the horse might be difficult to handle, she told herself.

Huffing a breath, she turned away from the window and pressed the wheel against the pattern again. He was a professional trainer, for heaven's sake. He'd all but grown up on a horse. He didn't need her to warn him that one might be dangerous.

Or did he?

Unsure of the answer, she dropped the wheel and hurried for the door.

When she didn't see any sign of Whit or the horse in the pen or the corral, she broke into a run. By the time she reached the barn, she was out of breath and convinced that War Lord had trampled Whit to death in the stall.

She skidded to a stop one step inside when she found Whit sitting on a bale of hay opposite the stall.

She pressed a hand against her chest to still her heart's frantic beating, giving herself a moment to calm, then started down the alleyway. "I thought I better warn you that he's a bit high-strung."

Whit didn't so much as glance her way. High-strung? he thought as he watched the horse nervously pace. This horse wasn't high-strung. He was a lit stick of dynamite just waiting to blow.

And he'd volunteered to defuse it.

With a sigh, he stood. "How much exercise does he get?"

Stopping in front of the stall, she wrapped a hand around one of the bars that formed the upper portion of the door and peered inside. "I usually let him out into his run each morning, then pen him inside at night."

The horse jerked his head up at the sound of her voice, then charged for the door, his teeth bared. Whit grabbed her arm and snatched her back before the horse could sink his teeth into her flesh.

Scowling, he released her. "I take it he doesn't like you."

She pursed her lips and frowned at the horse as she rubbed her arm. "No, and the feeling is mutual, I assure you."

"So how do you manage to get him out of his stall and back in again?"

With a shrug, she turned away. "Letting him out is the easy part. I open the door to the run from the outside, then duck between the fence railings, so he doesn't run over me when he races out."

She stooped to pluck a piece of hay from the bale Whit had been sitting on before continuing.

"Getting him back inside at night is a little trickier," she admitted as she twirled the straw between her fingers. "I discovered that if I fill his trough with feed, then hide, he'll usually go into the stall on his own. Once he's inside, I roll the outside door into place and lock him in.''

"And he continues to fall for that?'' he asked doubtfully.

She shrugged. "He likes to eat.''

"What do you feed him?''

She tossed the piece of straw away. "Same as Matt always did. Two pounds of crimped oats, two blocks of alfalfa and a half pound of sweet feed, both morning and night.''

He shook his head. "That's way too much feed for the amount of exercise he's getting. You need to cut the sweet feed out entirely and the oats in half. And don't give him any more alfalfa. Do you have any coastal?''

"I don't think so,'' she said uncertainly. "But I can get some at the feed store when I go into town.''

"No need. I've got plenty. I'll bring a couple of bales with me tomorrow.''

"So you're going to train him?''

He glanced her way, surprised that she'd ask. "I said I would, didn't I?''

"Well, yes, but...'' She lifted a hand, let it drop. "It's just that the other trainers I hired quit once they got a look at War Lord.''

He snorted a breath and turned his gaze to the horse. "I can understand why. He doesn't seem to care too much for humans.''

"No,'' she admitted. "Matt kept saying he was going to work with him, but he always found some excuse—'' She stopped midsentence, catching herself before saying something negative about her husband.

"Don't worry," he said wryly. "I'm aware of Matt's faults. He had great plans, but a lousy follow-through."

She didn't agree or disagree, but stooped to pick up a length of wire from the floor. As she straightened, she kept her gaze on her hands as she folded the wire back and forth, shaping it into a compact bundle.

"How long do you think you'll be here each day?" she asked after a moment.

"I'll need to leave today by two. Some days I'll be able to stay longer. Depends on the workload at my place. Is that a problem?"

She tossed the bundled wire into the trash can and dusted off her hands. "No. I spend most of the day in my workroom, so I doubt we'll get in each other's way." She turned to go, but called over her shoulder, "I'll be leaving soon to pick up my son from school. If you have any questions, you can leave me a note on the tack room door."

Resentment rose inside Whit as he watched her walk away. Leave her a note on the tack room door? Was that her way of telling him to stay away from the house?

He kicked at the bale of hay.

And why did she have to go and mention her son? He didn't want to think about her having a child. If he did, then he'd start thinking about what it took for her to have one.

And an image of her and Matt making love never failed to fill him with a blinding rage.

Three

———

Whit sat on an upended feed bucket, whittling what would become the handle for a quirt, while War Lord paced and pawed in the stall opposite him. This was the third day he had made the drive to Briggs to work with the horse, and he'd yet to enter the stall. But he knew better than to rush things. The time spent getting to know the horse and letting the horse get to know him would pay off in the end.

"Holdin' on to that tough-guy act has gotta be tiring," he said, continuing his one-sided conversation with the horse. "I know I'd be plumb tuckered out by now if I was the one doing all that pawing and posturing."

He paused to brush loose shavings from his thigh and stole a glance at the horse. Pleased to see that

War Lord had stilled and seemed to be listening, he went back to his whittling.

"Bet you'd like to stretch your legs a bit, wouldn't you? Run a hundred laps or so in that pretty green pasture beyond your run?"

He nodded as if the horse had responded in the affirmative. "Well, all that's keeping you from that pleasure is a surly attitude. Show a little courtesy to those who feed and care for you, and I'll see that you spend the morning kicking up your hooves in thick, green grass."

"War Lord can't go in the pasture."

Whit nearly fell off his bucket. When he'd righted himself, he glanced to his left and found a young boy standing not more than ten feet away. Though he'd never laid eyes on the child before, he knew he was looking at Melissa's son. The boy had inherited his mother's blond hair and brown eyes.

And nothing from his father, Matt.

Scowling, he pressed the blade of his knife against his thigh, closing it, then stood and slipped the tool into his pocket. "Who says I can't."

"Mom. She said that War Lord can't never go out in the pasture."

"And why is that?"

"'Cause if he does, she can't catch him and put him back in his run."

Closing one eye, Whit held up the piece of wood and studied its length for straightness. "I 'magine it'd be all right with your mom if I were to let him out, if I was the one to catch him and put him back into his stall."

"Nobody can catch War Lord if he don't want to be caught."

"Is that a fact?"

"Yep." The boy eased closer. "What's that you got?"

"This?" Whit asked, indicating the piece of wood. At the boy's nod, he said, "A handle for a quirt I'm whittling."

"Mom won't let me play with knives. Says I'm too little."

Whit angled his head and gave the boy a slow look up and down. "You are kind of short."

"Hey!" he cried indignantly. "I'm not short." He pulled himself up to his tallest, his shoulders almost touching his ears. "I'm the second biggest boy in my class."

Whit didn't want to like the kid, if for no other reason than he was Melissa's and Matt's son. But in spite of his predisposition, he found himself biting back a smile as he pulled his knife from his pocket. Thumbing open the blade, he sat on the bucket. "Then I guess she was referring to your age and not your size."

The boy scrunched up his nose, then sputtered a laugh. "Yeah. Okay. I get it." He ambled closer and bent over, bracing his hands on his knees as he watched Whit whittle. "What's your name?" he asked after a moment.

"Whit. What's yours?"

"Grady."

So, Melissa had given her son her maiden name,

he thought. Odd, considering her relationship with her father.

"My dad's dead."

Whit stiffened at the boy's blunt announcement. "Yeah," he said, and forced his hand into motion again. "I know."

"He went to heaven and can't never come home again."

Whit was at a loss as to what to say in reply. Thankfully Grady didn't seem to expect one from him.

"You ever been to heaven?" the boy asked curiously.

Whit shook his head. "Can't say that I have."

"Mom says it's a neat place. That the people who go there don't have to hurt anymore."

It was a simple explanation, but one Whit felt was more than adequate to soothe a little boy's fears and concerns.

"I imagine your mom's right." Hoping to distract the kid, he dragged the blade across his thigh, cleaning it, then turned the handle out, offering it to the boy. "Wanna try your hand at whittling?"

Grady's eyes grew round. "Can I?"

Before Whit had a chance to think better of his offer, Grady had scooted around between his spread knees and wriggled his bottom onto the edge of the bucket Whit sat on. The boy's hips were small, his body warm, and the scent he brought with him was the sour, wet-dog odor of a kid who'd spent an afternoon playing outdoors.

"What do I do now?" he asked expectantly.

Unaccustomed to dealing with kids, Whit inhaled a long breath. ''Well, first, I guess we'd better go over a few safety rules.''

''Like what?''

''Like, a knife is a weapon and can be dangerous if not properly used.'' He turned the blade up, exposing the sharp side. ''See how this side of the blade is narrower than the other? That's the working side and it's honed razor-sharp. Never, ever grab a knife by the blade. And if you're passing one to someone else, always fold the blade into the case before you do.''

Grady nodded.

''And never run with an open knife,'' Whit warned. ''If you should trip, you could fall on the blade and stab yourself.''

Grady glanced back over his shoulder to peer at Whit. ''Same as scissors, right?''

Whit nodded. ''Right.'' He slipped an arm around the boy and fitted the child's hand around the case. ''Keep your strokes light,'' he instructed as he guided the boy's hand and knife to the stick. ''You don't want to gouge the wood, just shave it. And always work the blade away from your body, never toward it.''

With his brow creased in concentration, Grady pushed the blade slowly along the wood.

''That's the idea,'' Whit encouraged.

Reaching the end of the stick, Grady released the breath he'd been holding. ''Did I do okay?''

Whit held the stick up to examine it. ''Couldn't have done better myself.''

Grady wriggled his bottom more firmly into the curve of Whit's legs. "Let's do it again."

Whit repeated the motions, fitting Grady's hand around the knife case and guiding the blade to the wood.

"Grady Jacobs! What do you think you're doing?"

Grady dropped the knife at the sound of his mother's voice, and shot guiltily to his feet. "I was just whittling, Mom. Whit said I could."

The look Melissa gave Whit could've peeled paint off the barn wall down to bare wood.

"Grady isn't allowed to play with knives," she informed him tersely.

Whit didn't appreciate her tone, nor did he care for the implication that he was an irresponsible adult. Picking up the knife, he pressed the dull side of the blade against his leg to close it and stood. "So he said. But he wasn't playing with the knife. I was teaching him how to use it."

She set her jaw. "*I'll* be the one to decide if and when Grady is ready to use a knife." She shifted her gaze to frown at Grady. "You're in big trouble, young man," she scolded. "Not only did you play with a knife when you know it's forbidden, you came to the barn alone."

"I wasn't alone," he argued. "Whit was here."

The kid had a point, Whit thought, but decided to keep his opinion to himself. He wasn't anxious to receive another dressing-down in front of the boy.

"Whether he was here or not isn't the issue. You are not allowed to come out to the barn alone." She lifted an arm and pointed a stiff finger toward the house. "Thirty-minute time-out in your room."

He scuffed a toe against the barn floor. "Ah, Mom. Do I have to?"

"Yes, you most certainly do. And if you argue with me about it, I'll make it an hour."

Dropping his chin to his chest, he stuffed his hands into his pockets and shuffled past her, his lips pushed out in a pout.

Whit waited until the boy was out of earshot. "Don't you think you were a little hard on the kid? It's not as if he intentionally disobeyed you. Like he said, I was here."

She snapped her head around and seared him with an accusing look. "And he was certainly safe with you, wasn't he? You gave him a knife to play with."

"He wasn't playing with it," he said in frustration. "I was teaching him how to use it."

"He's too young to use a knife."

"For God's sake, Melissa. He's a boy! At some point in his life, he's going to come in contact with a knife. Either a friend's or he'll buy his own. Wouldn't you rather he know how to properly handle one, than take a chance on him getting hurt?"

"I don't need you to tell me how to raise my son."

"No," he agreed. "I'm sure you know a lot more about child-rearing than I do. But I do know a little something about boys and the trouble they can get into, seeing as I was once one myself."

"He's my son," she said stubbornly. "I don't want him hurt."

"I doubt you do. But you can't protect him by

keeping him locked in a room all his life. At some point he's gonna want to go out into the world, and when he does, he's going to get a few bumps and bruises. You can't save him from them, no matter how badly you might want to. The best you can do is see that he's prepared.''

She opened her mouth as if to argue the point, then clamped it shut and stalked from the barn without another word.

Whit sat perched on top of the fence, the heels of his boots hooked over the rail below, watching as War Lord raced along the pasture fence line, his tail and mane flying. The horse had speed, there was no doubt about it. But whether a man would ever feel that speed beneath him had yet to be proven.

The horse had the surliest disposition Whit had ever come up against in all his years of training. Though he'd tried every trick in the book to calm the horse down, he'd yet to hit on one that worked.

He had made some progress, though. He could at least stand in the stall with the horse now. War Lord still wouldn't let him touch him, but the animal hadn't attempted to trample him to death or to bite his hand off, either, which Whit figured had to count for something.

But that something wasn't nearly enough.

He needed to finish the job. He wanted as far away from Melissa Jacobs as he could get. Not that she was making a pest of herself. In fact, he hadn't seen hide nor hair of her in three days. Not since the incident with Grady and the knife.

He was sure he'd overstepped his bounds in saying what he had to her, but he had no regrets about having stated his mind. A boy needed room to explore and grow, something the kid couldn't do with his mother hovering over him, monitoring his every move.

But their differences on child-rearing weren't why he wanted to distance himself from Melissa. He needed peace. The kind he'd known before Melissa had shown up at his place and asked him to train Matt's horse. To have that peace, he needed to forget her. Block her from his mind, just as he had seven years ago.

Scowling, he glanced over his shoulder toward the house. But it was damn hard to forget a woman when he was at her house seven days a week.

As if summoned by his thoughts, Melissa appeared in the open doorway of the garage, pushing a lawn mower ahead of her. The sight of her preparing to do yard work was unexpected enough to make him stare. Melissa didn't do yard work. Or at least the Melissa he'd known never had. Mike Grady wouldn't have allowed it. And why should he, when he had a full-time gardener on staff to do the dirty work?

But it wasn't the thought of Melissa doing yard work that held his gaze. Dressed in a pair of cut-off jeans and a baggy tank top, she exposed more flesh than she covered. He didn't begrudge her the skimpy clothing. Mowing was a sweaty job even if a person didn't consider the weather, and today it was hotter than Hades.

And judging by the heat that shot through his veins

as she stooped to check the oil and gas levels on the mower, the temperature was rising by the minute.

He told himself to look away, but his gaze refused to budge from the view of her heart-shaped buttocks.

After what seemed like forever, she straightened and dragged her palms across the seat of her shorts, then reached for the cord. She pulled, stumbling back a step with the release. When the engine failed to start, she frowned and reached to pull again. When the second attempt failed, she hunkered down beside the mower and fiddled with what he assumed was the spark plug. From his distance, he couldn't tell what part of the engine she was adjusting and really didn't care. The strip of skin exposed between the waist of her shorts and the bottom of her tank top was what held his attention.

At one time he'd known her body as well as he'd known his own. Had touched her in places that the cutoffs and tank top currently hid. But he didn't have to see her nude to remember the feel of her. He knew every curve, every swell, as well as the shivers or moans that could be drawn by touching each. He knew what it felt like to have her clinging to him, her face buried within the curve of his neck, her breath hot and moist against his skin. And he knew her scent when aroused, the soft, pliant yield of her body beneath the weight of his, the desperate arch of her spine as she strained to meet him.

Had she responded to Matt in the same way? he wondered.

Resentment burned through him at the unwanted thought, and this time he succeeded in tearing his gaze away. But before he could look away completely, she stood suddenly and looked toward the road. Curious to know what had caught her attention, he followed her gaze and saw a truck speeding toward the house, the flatbed trailer it pulled chased by a thick cloud of dust. He watched the truck brake to a stop on the drive and a man climb out.

Joe Banks? he thought in puzzlement, recognizing the owner of the local farm equipment dealership. What was Joe doing out here?

Then he remembered Woodrow mentioning a plow Melissa had sold a few weeks before, claiming she needed the money to make her mortgage. Was she so strapped for cash she was having to sell off more equipment? he wondered.

As the two started in his direction, he hopped down from the fence and headed inside the barn, telling himself that, if she was hard up for money, it was none of his business. He had enough problems to deal with without taking on any more of hers.

In the feed room, he plucked a bucket from a nail, scooped up a measure of oats and headed out again, taking the shortcut through War Lord's stall. As he stepped out into the sunshine, he heard an engine crank and glanced toward the equipment shed at his left. Melissa stood beside a tractor, her arms hugged around her waist, watching as Joe tested the tractor's hydraulic lift.

Surely she isn't going to sell the tractor, he thought in dismay. A person with any acreage at all needed a tractor to deal with the heavy work.

Again he made himself turn away, telling himself

that what she did was no concern of his. He'd almost made it to the end of the run, when the engine died and he heard Joe say, "I'll give you five thousand dollars."

Swearing under his breath, he dropped the bucket and vaulted over the fence.

Forcing a smile, he strode toward the equipment shed. "Hey, Joe. What brings you out this way?"

"Whit," Joe replied, tipping his hat in acknowledgment of the greeting. He nodded toward the tractor. "Came to take a look at the tractor Mrs. Jacobs has for sale."

Whit glanced at Melissa. "I didn't know you had a tractor for sale."

"Well, I—"

"Mind if I take a look?" Without waiting for her answer, he circled the tractor, pausing to kick a tire, then hunkered down and peered up at the engine from below. Straightening, he glanced over at her. "I'll give you seven-thousand."

"Now just a damn minute," Joe blustered indignantly. "I bought that tractor fair and square."

Whit kept his gaze fixed on Melissa. "Has he paid you for it yet?"

"Well, n-no," she stammered.

Whit shifted his gaze to Joe. "Then I guess it's still for sale. Want to offer her more than seven thousand? That's the current bid."

Joe glared at Whit, steam all but coming out his ears. "Seven-five," he stormed. "And not a penny more."

"I'll give her eight, which beats your offer of

seven-five. Unless you want to raise your bid, it looks like the tractor's mine.''

Joe's face turned an angry, mottled red, a strong indication that his blood pressure had risen to a dangerous level. ''Damn Tanners,'' he muttered under his breath as he stalked away. ''Throwing money around like it's theirs to burn. Ought to be a law against their kind.''

''Why did you do that?''

The anger in Melissa's voice had Whit whipping his head around to peer at her. ''Do what?''

She flung a hand in Joe's direction. ''Thanks to you, I'll never be able to sell him another piece of equipment.''

''The guy was robbing you! That tractor may be old, but it's worth a hell of a lot more than five grand.''

''It's worth what a person is willing to pay for it, and Joe was willing to give me five thousand dollars.''

''And I'm willing to give you eight.''

Flattening her lips, she turned for the house. ''I'm not selling my tractor to you.''

Stunned, for a second Whit could only stare, then he charged after her. ''And why the hell not?''

''Because you don't need a tractor.''

''Who says I don't?''

She swung around to face him. ''Do you have a tractor?''

He gestured to the one still parked in front of the barn. ''I just bought one, didn't I?''

''*Prior* to purchasing mine.''

Trapped, he tried not to squirm. "Well…yeah."

She turned on her heel and marched for the house. "That's what I thought."

He marched right after her. "What difference does it make if I own twenty tractors? I can buy another one, if I want."

She stopped at the lawn mower and bent to catch the cord in her hand. "I don't need your pity, Whit," she said, and gave the cord an angry yank.

The rope broke at the pressure and sent her stumbling back a step. She stared at the frayed end for three long seconds, then hiccuped a sob and dropped her face to her hands.

Whit didn't know whether to offer her his handkerchief or run like hell for the barn. He didn't want to feel sorry for her. But how could he feel anything less, when it was obvious that she'd reached the end of her rope, both literally and figuratively?

Heaving a sigh, he pulled his handkerchief from his back pocket and nudged it against the back of her hand. "There's no need to cry. I'll fix your mower for you."

She snatched her hands from her face. "It's not just the stupid lawn mower. It's everything! The pump on the well is acting up and it's time for Grady's annual dental exam. He's growing out of his clothes faster than I can buy him new ones and the insurance company called this morning and told me that if I didn't pay my premium before Friday, they're going to cancel my policy. And the property taxes are past due and I can't afford—"

She froze, her lips still shaped in the form of the last word, then turned away, her cheeks flaming.

"I have to pick up Grady," she said, and all but ran for the house.

Dental exams. Clothes. Insurance. Taxes. Food.

As Whit coaxed War Lord back into his stall, he couldn't stop thinking about the troubles Melissa had unintentionally shared with him. He was all too familiar with those kinds of worries as they were the same ones his mother had faced after his father had run off and left them.

He remembered as a kid lying awake at night, listening to his mother cry in the room next to his. In spite of his youth, he'd known it wasn't loneliness that caused her tears, although he suspected there was a measure of that in them, as well. It was the weight of the responsibilities she carried that had produced them. In retrospect, he wondered how she'd stood up beneath it all. Working full-time, while running a household and raising a child, was hard enough for any woman to do. But his mother had done it alone, without anyone with whom to share the burden.

She'd never once complained, though, about the hand life had dealt her. Not to Whit, at any rate. But he'd been aware of the weight she'd carried and, with each passing year, he'd tried to shift more and more of the workload off her shoulders and onto his. Chores the man of the house would have done, if they'd had one around. From the time he was big enough to push a mower, he'd done all the yard work. And he'd handled most of the household repairs, keeping their ancient washing machine in running condition and unclogging the plumbing when the pipes had stopped up. He'd even worked on her car a time or two. Necessity had provided him with one hell of an education, teaching him that there wasn't much that a length of baling wire or a roll of duct tape couldn't fix.

As he stepped out into the sunshine, he stopped to peer up at the house and the mower still parked on the drive. With the proper tools, he knew he could fix it. And, given the time, he could probably figure out what was wrong with her well pump, too. But the other problems she'd revealed to him couldn't be resolved with something as simple as a screwdriver or a wrench. They required money.

Whit wasn't a wealthy man by any stretch of the imagination, but he figured he could scrape together the cash she needed for the dental exam, clothes and insurance premium. And he could probably pay her property taxes without miring himself in debt.

But something told him she wouldn't accept money from him. Whether it was pride or just plain, old-fashioned stubbornness that would keep her from taking it, he wasn't sure.

Setting his jaw, he headed for the house. But he could fix her lawn mower. And he might even have time to work on the well pump, if he hadn't run out of daylight when he'd finished mowing her yard.

Of course, that would mean he'd be doing his own chores in the dark.

But the thought of working into the night didn't faze Whit. He figured it was better than tossing and turning in bed, which was what he'd been doing since Melissa had reentered his life.

While in town, Melissa stopped by the grocery store to pick up a gallon of milk, then by the library to check out books for Grady to practice his newly learned reading skills. Neither of the errands was all that pressing, but she'd wanted to drag out the trip as long as possible, hoping that Whit would be gone by the time she returned home. The thought of facing him again after the meltdown she'd suffered in his presence was too embarrassing to even think about.

Thanks to Grady and the hour it had taken him to choose which books he wanted to read, it was almost five when she turned off the highway and onto the road that led to the house. She stole a glance at the barn as she passed by and swallowed a groan when she saw that Whit's truck was still parked at its side.

"Hey!" Grady cried, straining against his seat belt to peer out the windshield. "Why's Whit mowing our yard?"

She snapped her gaze to the house and was shocked to find that not only was Whit mowing her yard, he was doing it half-dressed.

"I don't know," she murmured, her gaze riveted on his bare chest.

"Man, look at those muscles," Grady said.

She was trying her best not to, but was failing miserably.

"I bet he's stronger than Max Steel."

Max Steel was Grady's all-time-favorite superhero action figure, and while Melissa had to agree Max's "strong man" physique was certainly impressive, it was created by an artist's imagination. Whit's, on the other hand, was real, each muscle earned the old-fashioned way—through hard, physical labor.

Much too aware of Whit's bare chest, Melissa parked on the drive and killed the engine.

"Can I play with Champ?"

She murmured a distracted, "I guess so," as she groped blindly for her purse and the grocery sack.

"Yipee!" he shouted and jumped to the ground.

"Get your book bag," she said automatically as she stepped down from the opposite side.

With a groan, he reached back inside and dragged his bag from the floorboard, then slammed the door.

"Hey, Whit!" he yelled as he ran across the freshly mowed grass.

Whit lifted a hand in greeting, but kept mowing. He completed the last strip, then pushed the mower toward the garage and disappeared inside.

When he reemerged seconds later, he stopped on the drive to watch Grady and Champ romp. He had put his shirt back on, but hadn't bothered to button it. The afternoon breeze caught the tails and whipped them behind him. The hands he braced low on his hips kept them there, exposing a wide expanse of sweat-slickened chest.

The image he created standing there pulled a memory Melissa had locked away years ago. It had been a hot summer's day, the sun so bright it made your eyes ache. Anxious to see Whit, she'd taken a picnic lunch to the Tanner ranch, where she knew he was baling hay. Shirtless, he'd been driving a tractor when

he'd spotted her walking across the pasture. He'd
tugged his shirt from the back of the seat and
shrugged it on as he'd climbed down from the tractor.
He'd started to button it, then had stopped and opened
his arms. She'd dropped the basket and run toward
him, laughing as he'd scooped her up from the ground
and swung her around and around. She remembered
the smell of his skin, the heat the sun had burned into
it. And she remembered the taste of him as he'd
crushed his mouth over hers.

Heat pierced her low in her belly as she stared,
remembering. Although aware of its slow unfurling,
it took her a moment to recognize the sensation for
what it was.

How long had it been since she had felt anything
akin to desire? she wondered, awed by the sensation.
Months? Years? And had it ever been stirred by the
mere sight of a man?

Yes, she thought, gulping. This man.

As if he sensed he was being watched, Whit
glanced her way. Though a good twenty feet separated them, when their gazes met, his was like a
touch, brushing over her cheek, sliding over her lips,
grazing her breasts.

"Hey, Mom! Watch this!"

Startled by her son's voice, she tore her gaze from
Whit's in time to see Champ snag a ball from the air
and race back to drop it, dripping with saliva, at
Grady's feet.

She forced a smile. "That's really good, sweetheart," she called.

When he stooped to scrape the ball from the ground

to throw again, she glanced back at Whit and found he was still watching her. With the sun behind him, his face in shadows, it was impossible for her to read his expression or to gauge his thoughts. Was he remembering that day in the hay field, too? she wondered.

Furious with herself for even caring what he was thinking, she tore her gaze from his and started for the house. "Come on, Grady. It's time to wash up for dinner."

Grady dropped to his knees as Champ loped back with the ball. With an excited bark, Champ leaped against his chest, sending both boy and dog toppling back.

Laughing, Grady tried to dodge the dog's exuberant licks. "Is Whit going to eat with us?"

She fumbled a step at the unexpected question, then forced herself on. "I'm sure Whit already has plans for the evening."

"As a matter of fact, I don't."

Irritated that he hadn't taken the out she'd offered him, she turned and gave him a tight smile. "Then I hope you like red beans and rice, because that's what we're having."

The way Melissa was stabbing at the food in her bowl, Whit had a feeling she was imagining her spoon was a pin and her beans a voodoo doll shaped into his image. She wasn't happy that he'd taken Grady's innocent question and twisted it into a dinner invitation for himself.

But that was too damn bad.

Mowing gave a man time to think, and he'd spent the past couple of hours mulling over Melissa's financial situation, wondering if it was worse than he'd first thought. He'd finally decided that there was only one way to find out for sure and that was to ask her point-blank. Grady's backhanded dinner invitation had provided him the opportunity to do just that.

Unfortunately it seemed Grady was the only person at the table who seemed interested in talking to him. While Melissa had sat in stubborn silence, he and Grady had discussed everything from baseball to the crummy food served by the lunchroom staff at the kid's elementary school.

At the moment, the topic was pets.

"Champ's Mom's dog. But I'm gonna get a puppy all my own, aren't I, Mom?"

Her gaze on her bowl, Melissa replied vaguely, "Someday."

"Do you have a dog?" he asked Whit.

"Two. A blue heeler and a Heinz 57."

"What's a Heinz 57?"

Unsure how much a kid Grady's age would know about the mating of animals, Whit looked Melissa's way for help. When she kept her gaze on her bowl, he released a long breath. "Well," he began hesitantly, "I guess the best way to describe him is to say he's a dog of unknown parentage."

Grady wrinkled his nose. "What the heck does that mean?"

"It means," Melissa said impatiently, "that Whit doesn't know what breed of dog it is."

"Oh," Grady said slowly, then sank his teeth into

a wedge of cornbread. "What's your dogs's names?" he asked Whit as he chewed.

"The blue heeler I call Jocko, and the Heinz 57 answers to Mutt."

"Mutt?" Grady repeated, then sputtered a laugh. "That's a stupid name for a dog."

Whit lifted a shoulder. "He doesn't seem to mind it too much. So long as I feed him, I 'magine he'd answer to just about anything."

"I feed Champ," Grady said proudly. "That's one of my chores."

"Speaking of chores," Melissa said, and laid her napkin beside her plate, an obvious signal that she was bringing the meal to an end. "You've got a room to clean."

"Aw, Mom," he complained. "There's nothing wrong with my room."

She rose and carried her bowl to the sink. "Nothing that thirty minutes of cleaning won't cure."

Whit picked up his bowl and stood. He shot Grady a wink. "Bet it takes you longer than thirty minutes to clean your room."

His eyes sharpening at the challenge, Grady shot from his chair. "Bet it doesn't," he shouted as he raced for the stairs.

Biting back a smile, Whit began to gather the dishes from the table.

"You don't need to do that," Melissa said as she filled the sink with water. "I'm sure you've got work waiting for you at home."

"That I do," he agreed, and moved to set the dishes down on the counter to her left. "But you cooked. The least I can do is help with the dishes."

"Mowing my yard was payment enough."

This was the opening Whit had been waiting for.

His expression growing somber, he plucked a glass from the drain board and began to dry it. "How bad is it, Melissa?"

She bobbled the glass she was washing, then stuck it beneath the tap to rinse off the suds.

"It's really not all that bad. A few toys on the floor. Clothes that need to be hung up." She lifted a shoulder. "It shouldn't take him more than fifteen minutes."

When she reached to place the glass on the drain board, he laid a hand over hers and she snapped her gaze to his.

"I wasn't asking about Grady's room," he said quietly. "It's your financial situation that I'm concerned about."

Pursing her lips, she snatched her hand from beneath his and grabbed the stack of bowls, pushing them beneath the sudsy water with a little more force than was necessary. "I really don't think my financial situation is any of your business."

"No," he agreed. "But I'm making it mine." He opened a cabinet door and placed the glass inside, then glanced her way. "You can tell me yourself or I can find out on my own. It should be easy enough to do."

She hesitated a moment, then snatched her hands from the water and pushed past him, dragging her wet palms across the seat of her shorts.

"Outside," she said irritably as she slapped the screen door open. "I don't want my son hearing any of this."

Four

Melissa didn't stop until she'd reached a point in the backyard that she obviously considered far enough away from the house that Grady wouldn't overhear their conversation, then spun to face Whit. If he'd thought she was irritated with him before, that was nothing compared to the level of temper he was confronted with now. Her face was taut with anger, her body stiff with it.

"I'll tell you what you want to know, but what I say stays here," she said, jabbing a finger at the ground. "I don't want Grady hearing this from someone in town."

"All right," he said, though he wondered why she'd request such a thing, when it seemed the whole dang county was aware that Matt had left her in debt.

"Two months before Matt died, he signed a fifteen-year note, mortgaging the farm for three hundred and sixty-eight thousand dollars.''

Though Whit was stunned by the amount, he managed to keep the shock from his expression.

''Which leaves you with a monthly payment close to four grand,'' he said, quickly doing the math in his head.

At her nod, he wiped a shaky hand down his mouth then dropped it to a fist at his side. ''Dammit, Melissa! You knew that Matt didn't have a lick of sense when it came to handling money. Why'd you go and let him mortgage the homestead?''

''I didn't *let* him do anything,'' she returned angrily. ''The property was his, not mine.''

He tossed up his hands. ''Well, it's yours now. Mortgage and all. And what the hell did he need with that kind of money, anyway?'' He flung out a hand, indicating the empty pasture. ''It sure as hell wasn't to expand his herd, since there's not a damn cow in sight.''

She turned away, rubbing her hands up and down her arms as if chilled. ''No. Matt never cared for ranching.''

''Then why'd he borrow the money?''

''To pay off his gambling debts.''

''Gambling debts?'' he repeated, then shook his head. ''No way. Matt enjoyed a friendly wager every now and then, same as the next man. But that kind of gambling is nothing more than a form of recreation.''

''It may have started out that way, but gambling

became a compulsion, something he had no control over.''

Though Whit wanted to debate the issue with her, he knew that whether or not Matt was a compulsive gambler wasn't what was important. Not right now, anyway. It was getting Melissa out of the mess Matt had gotten her into that he had to focus on.

Rubbing a hand across the back of his neck, he paced away a few steps, trying to think of what money she might have available to her. ''What about life insurance?'' he asked, his mind seeking the most obvious solution first.

''He didn't have any.''

He dropped his hand to stare. ''But he had a wife and child. You'd think a man would be concerned about his wife and child?''

''He took care of us when he was here and would be still, if he'd lived.''

He tossed up his hands. ''I can't believe this. The man leaves you in debt up to your ears and you're defending him?''

She whirled to face him, her face taut with anger. ''Matt may have had his faults, but he was there for me when I needed him, unlike—''

When she didn't finish the statement, he frowned. ''Unlike who?''

She turned away, shaking her head. ''It doesn't matter. Not anymore.'' She started for the house. ''I need to go inside and check on Grady.''

Whit stared after her, his mind spinning with unasked questions. ''Melissa! Wait.''

She turned, hugging her arms at her waist. "What?"

"I gave you my word that I wouldn't repeat what you've told me and I won't. But there are plenty of people who know that Matt's left you in a bind. I've heard it from several different sources myself."

"I'm aware of the gossip."

"Well, I don't want you thinkin' it was me who blabbed, if Grady should hear about it."

"Grady knows that money is tight for us right now. What he doesn't know is *why*."

He wrinkled his brow in confusion. "You mean, no one knew about Matt's gambling?"

"Only myself and the person who made him the loan."

"He didn't borrow the money from a bank?"

"No."

"But there isn't a man around these parts with that kind of money to loan, other than—" He dropped his head back with a groan.

"Mike Grady," she finished for him. "And you're right. My father probably is the only individual who could afford to make a loan of that size."

If Melissa's situation could get any worse, Whit couldn't see how. As it was, she was standing beneath the gallows, a noose around her neck, and her father held the lever that could drop the floor out from under her at any given moment.

And her father would pull it, too. Whit didn't doubt that for a minute. Mike Grady was a cold-blooded, heartless man, who used his money and the power it gave him to control those around him—including his daughter.

Now Whit understood why Melissa hadn't gone to her father for help in the first place. Mike would probably have given her the money she needed. He might've even forgiven the note entirely, effectively wiping the slate clean.

But he wouldn't have done it without making her crawl first.

And it was that image that kept Whit awake most of the night.

He knew that Melissa wasn't out of the woods yet. There was still a strong possibility that she would have to ask her father for help. Selling off assets little by little was buying her some time, but it wasn't going to get her out of the hole Matt had dug for her. Not by a long shot.

From the conversations they'd had, it appeared to him that she was counting on War Lord to get her out of debt, and Whit knew that wasn't going to happen. War Lord was a valuable horse, he couldn't question that. But the horse's temperament cut his worth in two, if not by more.

With a sigh, he rolled to his side and punched his pillow up beneath his head. He was going to have to talk to her, he told himself. Warn her not to put all her hopes on the horse.

He didn't know how she'd react when he laid out the facts for her, but if it was true what they said about a person shooting the messenger of bad news, he figured he was as good as dead.

* * *

The next morning Whit bypassed the barn and drove straight to the studio, knowing that was where he'd find Melissa. After working on her place for over a week, he'd learned her habits well enough to know that she went there each morning after getting Grady off to school.

Even though he knew warning her about War Lord was the right thing to do, by the time he reached the building his hands were slick with perspiration and his stomach knotted with dread.

Although the door stood open, he rapped his knuckles against the facing, not wanting to startle her as he had the first time he'd visited her studio.

Bent over a box, she glanced up, then slowly stood. "Is something wrong?"

He dragged off his hat and stepped inside. "No," he said, then amended, "At least I hope not." He turned his hat between his hands, trying to think of the kindest way in which to break the news to her. "It's about War Lord," he began.

The color drained from her face. "Please don't tell me you're going to quit."

He shook his head. "No, I'm going to finish the job. But if you're thinking that horse is going to bring enough money to pay off your loan, you're wrong. His bloodlines are good, there's no doubt about that. And he's got speed. I've seen him run. But even broken to a saddle, he won't bring anywhere near the three-hundred-plus grand you need."

She released the breath she'd been holding and stooped to pick up the box, looking relieved.

"I never thought he would," she said as she moved

to set the box on her worktable. "But the price he brings will give me some breathing room."

"How do you figure that?"

She picked up a pen and jotted something down on a pad. "I've done my research. I've tracked the sales of every colt out of War Lord's sire, as well as those from the mare that bore him. On average, they've each sold for well over one hundred thousand dollars."

She tore the page from the pad and placed it inside the box. "Even if War Lord brings less than the average," she continued as she folded over the box's flaps and sealed it, "it won't be by much. But whatever he nets should be sufficient to supplement my income, until I can grow my business to a point where it will support Grady and myself."

Whit glanced at the boxes scattered around the room and the weird assortment of items protruding from them, and wondered how she thought she could make a living selling stuff fashioned from junk. Granted, the items were marketable. He remembered Macy saying that Melissa's designs flew out of her store faster than she could slap a price tag on them. But Melissa was only one person. There was no way in hell she could make enough stuff to support both herself and a child.

But he didn't think it wise to share his doubts with her. If he did, she'd probably take it as an insult toward her work.

As she moved to pick up another box, he quickly slapped his hat over his head and crossed to take it from her. "Here. I'll get that."

She turned a shoulder, blocking him. "I can do it."

They played a brief game of tug-of-war before she finally released the box with a huff of breath. "Okay. Fine. Take it." She pointed toward the door and the boxes already stacked to its left. "Put it over there with the others."

"Where are you taking all this?" he asked as he angled the box on top of the stack.

"There's an antique and craft show at Barton Creek Mall in Austin tomorrow. I've rented a space."

Stifling a sigh, he turned and saw that she was busy writing on the pad again. "Listen, Melissa. If you need to borrow a little money to get by on—"

"No," she said, cutting him off before he could make the offer. "I don't want your money."

He flattened his lips in frustration. "Whether you want it or not, isn't the point. You need it and it just so happens I've got some to spare."

"I'm not borrowing money. Matt did enough of that, as it is."

"Consider it a gift, then." He chuckled, trying to make light of the offer. "Hell, you'd be doing me a favor by taking it. If it stays in the bank much longer, I'll probably just buy another horse and God knows I've got enough now to outfit the Canadian Mounties."

"No, Whit."

Hearing the stubbornness in her refusal, he scowled. "Okay," he said as he turned to leave. "But if you change your mind, all you gotta do is give me the word and the money is yours."

He'd almost made it to the door when her voice stopped him. "Whit?"

He glanced back over his shoulder. "Yeah?"

Her lips trembled in the first smile she'd graced him with in seven years. "Thanks. Matt was lucky to have a friend like you."

Whistling, Whit strode inside the barn, nabbing the feed bucket from the nail as he passed by. In the feed room he scooped out a measure of oats, then headed back out. Hearing a rustle of movement in the loft overhead, he stopped and frowned, listening.

Mice, he decided, and made a mental note to tell Melissa she needed to get herself a cat. Continuing on to War Lord's stall, he dumped the oats into the horse's swing-out feeder, then added a square of hay before latching the door into place.

As he lifted the bucket to hang on the nail again, a shower of dust and straw rained down on his hat from above. Frowning, he dropped the bucket handle over the nail, then hooked a boot onto the bottom rung of the loft ladder and climbed up.

Poking his head above the opening, he peered around, looking for any signs of mice. He didn't see any mice, but what he did see made him bite back a smile. The soles of a child-size pair of sneakers protruded from between two bales of hay. Knowing he'd probably find Grady on the other end, he heaved himself up and moved to peer over the stack of bales.

Grady looked up at him sheepishly. "Hi, Whit."

"Hi, yourself. What are you doing hiding up here?"

Grady pressed a finger against his lips. "Shh. I don't want Mom to find me."

"Doesn't your mother have a rule about you coming to the barn alone?"

He scrunched up his nose. "Yeah. But she's making me go to Austin with her and sit in the boring mall all day. I'm hiding, so I don't have to go."

"Do you really think she'll leave without you?"

"Maybe," Grady said, though he sounded doubtful. "She said it's real important and she can't be late."

Whit cocked his head, listening. "Hear that?" he asked. "Sounds like your mother is headed this way." He offered Grady a hand. "Come on, cowboy. Time to face the music."

Reluctantly, Grady allowed Whit to haul him up and over the bale of hay he was hiding behind.

"Think she'll be mad at me?" he asked uneasily.

Whit stepped to the side, allowing Grady to precede him down the ladder. "I can almost bet on it."

His expression glum, Grady climbed down. Whit followed. At the bottom, Grady slipped his hand into Whit's and looked up at him.

"Will you go with me? She might not yell as loud if you're there."

The hand clasped in Whit's was small, but the warmth it contained did something to his chest. He gave him a nod. "Lead the way, cowboy."

As they stepped out into the sunshine Grady stopped short. "Uh-oh," he murmured. "There's Mom."

Whit had already spotted Melissa hurrying toward the barn, her forehead creased with worry.

Seeing them, she broke into a run. "Grady Jacobs," she scolded. "Where have you been? I've been looking all over for you."

Grady eased closer to Whit's side. "I don't want to go to Austin."

Melissa huffed an exasperated breath. "Well, I'm sorry, but you don't have a choice." She extended her hand. "Now come on. We're going to be late."

He tucked his face behind Whit's arm. "Please, Mom? Couldn't I stay here with Whit? I'll be good, I swear."

"I'm going to be gone all day, Grady," she said impatiently. "Whit will be gone before I get back. Now come on."

"He could tag along with me," Whit offered, then glanced down at Grady and shot him a wink. "I've been needing me a gate opener."

Grady's eyes brightened. "Could I, Mom? *Please?*" he begged.

"You don't need to worry," Whit assured her. "I'll keep a close eye on him."

"I don't know," Melissa replied hesitantly. "You'd have to feed him lunch and dinner. And what if he gets tired? He gets really grumpy when he's tired."

"I 'magine we can grab a bite to eat when we pass through town. And if he gets tired, he can sack out on the couch at my house."

Melissa caught her lip between her teeth as she looked from Whit to Grady, then dropped her shoulders in defeat. "Oh, all right," she said as she dug in her purse for a pen and paper. She jotted down a number and offered the slip of paper to Whit. "Here's my cell number. Call me if you have any problems."

"Do you want to pick him up at my place when you're done or would you rather I bring him home?"

She hesitated a moment, then tugged a key off her key ring. "It would probably be better if you brought him home. That way, if I'm late, he can go on to bed."

The heels of Grady's sneakers thumped against the sides of the booth with each excited swing of his legs. Grinning, he backhanded a streak of mustard from his chin. "This hamburger's really good."

Whit popped his last French fry into his mouth. "Yep. Miss Leonard makes a mean burger, all right."

"Are we going to your house next?" he asked.

"In a bit. First I need to stop in at my brother's Western store and pick up a bridle I ordered."

"You have a brother?"

Whit nodded. "Four to be exact."

"Wow," he murmured, he eyes round in awe. "That's a lot."

Chuckling, Whit nodded. "Yeah. I suppose it is."

Grady picked up his chocolate shake and took a long pull on the straw, then backhanded the froth from his mouth. "I don't have any brothers or sisters. One time I asked Mom if I could have a little brother and she said it wasn't in the stars." He tipped his head to the side and gave Whit a curious look. "What does stars have to do with me getting a brother?"

"I suppose she was saying that you weren't meant to have one."

"Like it wasn't in God's plan or something?"

"Yeah. Something like that." Before Grady could ask any more questions, Whit reached for his hat. "You 'bout ready?"

Grady quickly scooted from the booth. "You bet."

Whit dropped a twenty-dollar bill on the table, then rose, stuffing his wallet into his back pocket as he walked with Grady to the door.

Once on the sidewalk, Grady slipped his hand into Whit's. Again, Whit felt that same odd sensation in his chest.

"What's your brothers's names?" Grady asked as they walked down the sidewalk to the Western store on the next block.

"Ace is the oldest. Then there's Woodrow and Ry. Rory, he's the one who owns the Western store, he's the youngest."

"Younger than you?"

"No. Actually, he's almost a year older than me."

"Then how come you said he was the youngest?"

"Because he's the youngest of the Tanner brothers." Realizing he was probably confusing the boy, he explained, "They're not my real brothers. They're stepbrothers."

"What are stepbrothers?"

Whit blew out a breath. "Well, you see, my mother married their father and their father adopted me, which is how I got the Tanner name."

"What was it before?"

"Grainger."

Grady grew quiet as if thinking about that, then asked, "Do you have any kids?"

Whit snorted a laugh. "No. Can't say as I do."

"That's too bad," Grady said with regret.

"Why's that?"

"If you did, you could marry my mom and I could have stepbrothers same as you."

Whit faltered a step, then released Grady's hand to open the door to the Western store. "Yeah," he murmured. "That's a shame, all right."

As they stepped inside, Rory was approaching from the rear of the store. Seeing Whit, he stopped and beamed a smile. "Well, look what the cat dragged in," he said, then gestured at Grady. "Who's the squirt tagging along behind you?"

Grady pushed out his lips. "I'm no squirt."

"Watch it," Whit warned his stepbrother. "He doesn't take kindly to remarks about his size."

Rory hunkered down to Grady's height and extended a hand. "No harm meant. Do you have a name?"

Though reluctant, Grady accepted Rory's hand. "Grady Jacobs," he muttered.

Rory glanced up at Whit in surprise. "This is Melissa's kid?"

At Whit's nod, Rory looked back at Grady and smiled. "Well, I'll be darned. Did you know your mama's daddy and mine were friends?"

"I don't like Granddaddy Mike. He's mean."

Rory choked a laugh, then stood, clapping a hand on Grady's back. "Smart kid," he said to Whit, then asked, "So what are you two up to?"

Whit kept an eye trained on Grady as the boy wandered off to admire the boots lined up on a shelf. "Dropped by to see if that bridle I ordered came in."

Rory shook his head. "Not yet. I expect another shipment tomorrow, though. Want me to give you a call when it comes in?"

"Yeah. That'll work." He dropped his gaze to the scuffed tennis shoes Grady wore and frowned, remembering Melissa telling him the kid was outgrowing his clothes faster than she could buy them.

He tipped his head toward Grady. "You got any boots his size?"

"Boots, jeans, shirts. Whatever a kid needs, I stock it."

Whit started toward Grady. "What about hats? I'm thinking he could use one. And a belt, too. And is the guy around who does the tooling? I want his name carved into the leather."

Melissa was relieved to see Whit's truck parked on her drive when she returned home. Exhausted after standing on her feet all day at the craft show, she climbed from her car and brushed her hair back from her face to look at the house. Only two lights appeared to be on. The one above the sink in the kitchen and the lamp in the den. Anxious to make sure that all had gone well in her absence, she crossed to the back door. As she stepped into the kitchen, she half expected to find it in a mess. But the counters were clean, as was the table, and what dishes had been used were washed and stacked in the drainer. She could hear the sound of the TV coming from the den and knew that's where she'd find Whit and Grady.

She stopped short just inside the room, placing a hand over her heart at the tender scene that greeted her. Whit sat in the recliner, his head tipped back and one arm draped loosely around Grady, who sat on his lap. Both were sound asleep.

She didn't know what she'd expected to find when she returned home, but it certainly wasn't *this*. They looked so peaceful, so *comfortable* together, that she had to blink back unexpected tears.

Tiptoeing quietly across the room, she stopped in front of them and simply stared. Grady had on his Scooby-Doo pajamas and looked as if he was fresh from a bath. Whit was wearing the same clothes he'd had on that morning, with the exception of his boots, which lay in a heap on the floor. His stockinged feet formed an open-ended V on the recliner's footrest and Grady's bare feet dangled from between his sprawled legs.

Reaching out, she laid a hand lightly on Whit's shoulder.

"Whit?" she whispered.

He blinked open his eyes, slowly brought her into focus, then closed them again with a groan.

Biting back a smile, she reached for Grady. "Here. Let me have him and I'll take him up to bed."

He tightened his arm around Grady. "No. I will."

He forced open his eyes, blinked twice, as if to wake himself, then pressed his heels against the footrest and slowly lowered it. Gathering Grady into his arms, he stood and tipped his head toward the stairs. "You lead the way."

With Whit following, Melissa climbed the stairs and turned into Grady's room. She switched on the bedside lamp and peeled back the bedcovers, then stepped out of the way, giving Whit room to lay Grady down.

Grady rolled to his side, with a sigh, and curled into a ball. Her smile tender, Melissa pulled the covers over him and leaned to press a kiss to his temple. As she reached to switch off the lamp, she noticed the pile of clothes on the floor and cut a questioning look at Whit.

He lifted his shoulder in a shrug. "We picked up a few things while we were in Rory's store."

Unsure how to respond to the kindness, she switched off the lamp and led the way back downstairs. "I hope Grady didn't talk you into buying all those things."

"It was my idea, not his." Whit dropped onto the recliner, picked up a boot and tugged it on. "I figured if he was going to cowboy with me today, he needed to dress the part. And, yes," he said before she could ask, "he thanked me for them."

She smiled softly. "Then I'll add my thanks to his. That was very kind of you."

He stood, stomping his feet down into his boots. "It was no big deal. Rory gives me a pretty hefty discount on everything I buy."

As he explained that to her, he was stuffing the tail of his shirt into his jeans, and the movement was so utterly masculine, so familiar, she felt heat rush to her cheeks.

Embarrassed by her reaction, she stooped to pick up one of Grady's action figures from the floor.

"How'd the craft sale go?" he asked as he plucked his hat from the sofa.

Straightening, she sighed tiredly. "Exhausting, but profitable."

He turned his hat in his hands, as if reluctant to leave. Oddly she felt the same way.

"Would you like something to drink?" she asked. "I don't have anything to offer stronger than lemonade, but it's fresh. I made it this morning."

He hesitated a moment, as if he might accept the invitation, then shook his head. "No, you've had a long day and are probably anxious to get to bed." He headed for the door. "I'll see you tomorrow."

Not wanting him to leave just yet, but uncertain why, she followed. "Whit?"

He turned around so fast, she had to throw out a hand to keep from slamming into his chest. Their gazes met and she froze, painfully aware of the pads of muscle that lay beneath her palm and the heat that seeped into it. It was all she could do to keep from melting against his chest and absorbing the warmth and comfort she'd once found there.

"Whit, I—"

Before she could say more, he lowered his face and touched his lips to hers. Tears filled her eyes. She'd forgotten how tender a kiss could be, how sweet. Though this wasn't her purpose in following him to the door, she realized now how badly she'd wanted his kiss, how long she'd yearned for his touch.

As if sensing her need, he shifted to wrap an arm at her waist and pull her closer. Heat spilled through her as he deepened the kiss, holding her body against his. Lips, chests, abdomens, thighs. Each place his body touched hers tingled with awareness.

Much too soon, he withdrew and she opened her eyes to find his gaze on her and his forehead furrowed in concern. Lifting a hand, he swept a thumb beneath her eye, catching a tear that had escaped.

"I'm sorry," he murmured. "I didn't mean to upset you."

Moved by the regret in his voice, she shook her head. "No," she said, finding her voice. "You didn't upset me. It's just that I—"

She dropped her gaze, unable to tell him that the tears were tears of joy, not anger or hurt. But the feelings were too unexpected, too confusing for her to share.

Lifting her head, she forced a smile. "Thanks for keeping Grady for me today."

"He was no problem."

She gave him a bland look. "You forget who you're talking to. I'm his mother. I know what a handful he can be. There are times when I'm tempted to stick an apple in his mouth just to get a moment's peace and quiet."

Chuckling softly, he nodded. "He does tend to ask a lot of questions."

"I don't know where he comes up with them all."

"It does make a person wonder."

Silence settled between them and Melissa couldn't think of anything else to say. Obviously he suffered the same problem.

He settled his hat over his head and reached for the doorknob. ''Well, I guess I better be going.''

''Thanks again,'' she said.

''Don't forget to lock the door.''

''I won't.''

Then he was gone.

Melissa stood for a moment, staring at the closed door, fighting the urge to yank it open and call him back.

Taking in a shaky breath, she made herself twist the lock and turn away.

Five

Whit lay on the hood of his truck, his back braced against the windshield and his hands folded behind his head, staring up at the sky. The night was clear and the stars studding the blue-black sky appeared so close he was sure he could reach out and scoop up a handful, if he'd had a need for them. Though he was bone-dead tired and his house and bed lay not more than a hundred feet away, he wasn't ready to go inside yet. He had too much on his mind.

He still couldn't believe that he'd kissed Melissa, didn't know what had possessed him to do such a crazy fool thing. He'd been on his way out the door and would've made it, too, if she hadn't called his name. Yet it wasn't her voice that had made him kiss her. It was the feel of her hand on his chest and the expectant look in her eyes as she'd gazed up at him that had drawn his mouth down to hers.

He wanted to claim insanity, swear on a Bible that he'd never meant to so much as lay a hand on her. But he'd be lying, if he did. He'd wanted to kiss her for days now, though he wasn't even aware that need existed until his lips had touched hers.

Now all he could think about was kissing her again. What was worse, his thoughts were quickly running toward doing more than just kissing. He wanted to stroke the heat from her body, feel the arch of her spine as she reached for him, hold her in his arms while she came apart beneath him, sleep with her nestled against his side.

And that kind of thinking was just damn crazy. He'd spent the last seven years despising her for what she'd done to him. What man in his right mind would set himself up for that kind of pain again?

Therein lay the problem, he thought glumly. Crazy or not, he was already thinking of how he could get her alone again, imagining the different ways he'd please her and the pleasure she would give him in return.

Was it just sex he wanted from her? he asked himself honestly. Considering his current lustful thoughts, it was a possibility, but he seriously doubted that was the full reason. Sex had never been a big priority with him. He'd gone months without it and could do so again, if need be.

She'd responded to him. He hadn't imagined that. He'd felt the soft yield of her lips beneath his, the desperate dig of her fingers as she'd clung to him.

He'd tasted the need in her, sensed the heat that had sizzled a level below.

Slow, he told himself. That's what this situation called for. He wouldn't charge full-speed into another relationship with her. He'd take things slow and easy. Find out what had happened before. What had made her turn to Matt when she'd promised her heart to him.

Then he'd see what, if anything, the future might hold for them.

The screen door slapped closed with a bang as Grady raced into the kitchen, his face red and his chest heaving.

"Whit's here," he said breathlessly. "And he's pulling a trailer with a big white horse in it. Can I go down to the barn and see it?"

Plucking a dish towel from the counter, Melissa dried her hands as she strained to peer out the window over the sink, knowing she couldn't allow Grady to go to the barn alone. Not without setting a precedent that he would capitalize on in the future.

But the thought of going with him and having to face Whit again filled her with dread. She'd spent half the night worrying about the kiss they'd shared…and the other half dreaming about it.

"Why's he bringing a horse over here?" she asked, stalling.

"I don't know!" he cried in frustration. "Can I *please* go down to the barn and see?"

Melissa dropped the towel in resignation and held out her hand. "Okay. But I'm going with you."

Grady all but dragged her to the back door and across the yard. Melissa hurried to keep up. By the time they reached the barn, Whit had backed his trailer to the gate of the corral and was climbing down from his truck.

Grady tugged free of her hand and raced ahead to greet him. "Hey, Whit!" he yelled.

Grinning, Whit ruffled Grady's hair. "Hey, yourself, cowboy."

"Can I pet the horse?" Grady asked.

"I suppose so." Whit scraped him up under one arm, holding him like a sack of potatoes as he lifted him level with the trailer's open window.

Giggling, Grady rubbed the horse's nose.

"Careful, Grady," Melissa warned as she caught up with them. "The horse might bite."

Whit glanced her way, then let his gaze drift to her mouth. She felt the heat all the way to her toes.

"No need to worry about Molly biting," he assured her. "She's gentle as a lamb."

Praying that her legs would continue to support her, Melissa stretched to her toes to peer inside the trailer. Her eyes widened in surprise. "Oh, my. She's so… big."

Chuckling, Whit set Grady back on his feet. "Go ahead and say it. She's fat and ugly to boot."

She dropped back down on her heels and pursed her lips. "I was trying not to hurt her feelings."

"Mol knows she's fat. Don't you, girl?" he said, giving the mare an affectionate pat.

Melissa eased closer and dragged a knuckle over the horse's nose. "Why did you bring her here?"

"Well, I had this idea last night while I was puzzlin' over the problem with War Lord. It occurred to me that he might be lonely, so I brought Molly over to see if she'd have a calming effect on him. I'm not sure if it'll work, but I figured it was worth a try."

"You mean, Molly's gonna stay here?" Grady asked, obviously thrilled at the prospect.

"For a while," Whit told him.

"But aren't you worried that War Lord might hurt her?" Melissa asked in concern.

"No need to worry about Molly. She can take care of herself. She's pretty much bombproof, which is why I chose her for this job. If any horse can put up with War Lord's sour disposition, it's ol' Mol. Now, if y'all will step back outta the way, I'll unload her and introduce the two of 'em."

As Whit started for the rear of the trailer, Grady fell in behind him, but Melissa caught his hand and dragged him back to hold against her side.

Whit unlatched the trailer door and swung it wide, then reached inside and gave the old mare a slap on her rump. "Come on, Molly," he coaxed. "Out you go."

As the horse backed from the trailer, he clipped a lead rope to her halter, then swung the door closed and slid the latch into place. Leading the mare behind him, he crossed to the center of the corral.

After removing her halter, he began to back away. "Now wait right here," he instructed the horse. "I've got somebody I want you to meet."

Slinging the halter over his shoulder, he headed for War Lord's run. From inside the barn, Melissa could hear the horse snorting and thrashing around and prayed that Whit knew what he was doing.

She watched him slide back the bar that held the stall door in place, then quickly jump back out of the way as War Lord charged out, his head bowed and his nostrils flared. The horse's rear hooves arced out in a kick, missing Whit's arm by inches as he raced down the run and out into the corral.

Spotting Molly, the stud skidded to a stop. He tossed back his head and snorted, pawing the ground. Molly gave him a bored look, then turned her head away. Obviously insulted, he reared, then raced toward her.

Melissa held her breath as the stud slid to a stop mere inches from the mare. His head high, the stud pranced around the mare, sniffing. After circling her several times, he stopped and nudged her side with his nose. Turning, he nickered, as if to say, "Follow me," and trotted out to the pasture. Molly watched him for a moment, then followed at a much slower pace.

Whit gave Melissa and Grady a thumbs-up.

"Looks as if War Lord has himself a friend," he said as he rejoined them at the trailer.

"I can't believe that," Melissa said in amazement. "I honestly thought he intended to hurt her."

"If I'd brought a stud, instead of Mol, we probably would've had a fight on our hands. But Mol doesn't present a threat to War Lord, which is why I chose her for the job."

"Can I ride Molly?" Grady asked.

Whit looked to Melissa for permission. "That's up to your mother."

"Maybe later," she said. "For now, I think we need to give her and War Lord time to get used to each other."

"That's probably best," Whit agreed. "I'd planned to get a stall ready for Molly, then head back to my place and do my chores. When I come back later this afternoon to feed, he can ride then."

"Can I help you get the stall ready?" Grady asked.

Again, Whit looked to Melissa for permission.

"Won't he be in your way?" she asked uncertainly.

"Nah," Whit replied, then shot Grady a wink. "In fact, I could probably use an extra set of muscles."

Grady slipped his hand into Whit's and grinned up at him. "I've got big muscles. Wanna see?"

The sound of a car approaching pulled Melissa's gaze to the road. Her stomach knotted at the sight of the black Mercedes that was racing toward the barn at an unusually high speed.

She wanted to run and hide—or, at the very least, to hide Whit. Before she could do either, the car skidded to a stop beside Whit's truck and her father climbed out. By the red flush on his face and the fury with which he slammed the door, she knew this wasn't a social call.

Leveling an accusing finger at Whit, he strode toward them. "What are *you* doing here?"

Not wanting her son to witness the scene she feared was about to take place, Melissa said, "Go to the house, Grady."

"But, Mom," he complained.

Whit released Grady's hand and gave him a gentle push. "Do like your mother says," he said quietly.

Grady looked up at Whit, then dipped his chin to his chest and shuffled off toward the house.

Melissa waited until he was out of earshot, then turned to her father, her face taut with fury. "Who I invite onto my property is none of your business."

Ignoring her, Mike Grady kept his gaze locked on Whit. "I told you once to stay away from my daughter. Don't make me have to tell you again."

Melissa's mouth dropped open in shock. "You did what?"

"When he came sniffin' around seven years ago, I told him then I wouldn't have my daughter hanging out with white trash."

Her mouth closed with an angry click of teeth. "Don't you dare refer to Whit as white trash," she said furiously.

"Why not? That's what he is. His mother was nothing but a two-bit waitress from the wrong side of the tracks."

With a low growl, Whit lunged, grabbing Mike by the throat and shoving him up against the side of the trailer.

Paralyzed, Melissa watched her father's face turn red, his eyes bulge. Afraid that Whit was going to kill him, she leaped forward to grab his arm.

"Stop it!" she cried as she tried to break his hold. "Stop, before you kill him."

Something in her voice must have penetrated his

anger, because he gave Mike one last shove, smacking his head against the trailer, then dropped his hand.

"You can say what you want about me," he said through clenched teeth, "but you leave my mother out of this."

Mike straightened, his lip curled in a snarl. "I don't take orders from you or anybody else."

"You'll take one from me," Melissa said furiously. "You owe Whit an apology and I expect you to give him one right now."

"I don't owe that boy nothing. I ran him off once, and by God I'll do it again."

"I didn't run anywhere," Whit said angrily.

"Left town, didn't you?" her father challenged. "Good thing, too. Gave Melissa the time she needed to come to her senses and realize what her life would be like if she was to marry white trash such as you. Had her running back to Matt so fast, it would've made your head spin to watch."

"No," Melissa said, shaking her head in denial. She turned to Whit. "That's not true. I swear it's not true."

He stared at her a long moment, then turned away.

"Whit!" she cried, and started after him. "Wait!"

Her father grabbed her arm, yanking her back.

"Let him go," he growled. "Like I told you before, that boy's nothing but trash."

Furious, she snatched her arm from his grasp. "I've always known that you were cruel and heartless, but I never dreamed that you'd intentionally do something to hurt me."

"Hurt you?" he repeated incredulously. "Hell, I saved you from a life of misery."

"No," she argued. "You created one for me."

He narrowed his eyes and leveled a finger at her. "Now don't you go blaming me for your problems with Matt. He was a good boy. Did the right thing by marrying you. And he'd have made you a good husband, too, if you'd allowed him his full marital rights to your bed."

She pointed at his car, her entire body shaking with fury. "Get off my land."

"Your land?" he repeated, then snorted a breath. "I think you're forgetting who holds the deed on this property."

"I haven't forgotten," she replied coldly. "You won't let me forget. But as long as I make the payments, *I'm* the one who'll decide who comes and goes." She punched the air with her finger, indicating his car. "And you're leaving."

When Melissa stepped into the house, Grady was waiting for her at the door.

"Whit left," he said, his lip quivering. "I saw him go. Did Grandpa Mike make him leave?"

Though she would've preferred to go to her room and cry for three hours straight, she knew Grady deserved some kind of explanation. Gathering him against her side, she walked him into the den.

"No, honey," she said as she sank to the sofa and pulled him onto her lap. "Whit left because he wanted to."

Tears filled his eyes. "But me and him were going to get a stall ready for Molly. He said so."

She tugged him back against her and tucked his head beneath her chin. "I know, sweetheart."

"Grandpa Mike made him leave, didn't he?"

"Whit and your grandfather don't get along very well," she hedged.

He sat up, his hands balled into fists. "I hate Grandpa Mike!"

"Oh, baby," she soothed, stroking a hand over his hair. "You don't mean that."

"Yes, I do! And he hates me, too. He acts like I don't even have a name."

"He knows your name."

"He doesn't never say it. He calls me *boy,* not Grady. And when he talks to you about me, he always says *that boy of yours,* instead of my name."

Her heart broke a little, because she knew what he said was true. Her father's refusal to acknowledge her son was just one of the many ways he'd devised to hurt her. But she hadn't realized that Grady had been aware of the slight, as well.

Defending her father was the last thing she wanted to do, but she wouldn't let his actions hurt her son.

"I'm sure he doesn't mean anything by it," she said quietly. "Grandpa Mike is big and gruff and doesn't always think about what he says or how it might hurt someone's feelings."

Sniffing, Grady curled against her chest and laid his head on her shoulder. "He should."

Because she agreed wholeheartedly, Melissa remained silent, combing her fingers through his hair.

"Is Whit going to come back this afternoon?"

"I don't know."

His tears started again. "He promised I could ride Molly when he came back to feed."

She pressed a kiss against the top of his head. "I know he did, sweetheart. But sometimes we can't keep the promises we make."

"You always do."

Melissa closed her eyes against the pain that ripped through her, knowing there was one promise she'd made that she hadn't kept. She'd promised Whit that she would love him forever.

"No, Grady," she murmured sadly. "I've broken promises, too."

Melissa sat in front of her bedroom window long after she'd turned out the lights, trying to think what she should do. Her heart cried out for her to go to Whit, to tell him that she'd never known that her father had told him to stay away from her. That she was unaware that her father was responsible for him leaving town.

But what good would it do now? she asked herself hopelessly. No matter how badly she wanted to, she couldn't change the past. What was done, was done. She'd married Matt, had a child. Nothing she could do or say would change any of that.

A set of headlights appeared on the road, startling her. She watched the twin beams of light slice through the darkness as the vehicle swung onto the lane that led to the barn. Recognizing the truck as Whit's, she slowly rose, her heart pounding behind her breasts.

Knowing that she had to talk to him, if for no other reason than to apologize for the things her father had said, she grabbed her robe and hurried for the door, shrugging it on.

Once outside, she broke into a run, the hem of her robe soaking up the dew that covered the grass. Just as she stepped inside the barn, the overhead lights flashed on and she stopped for a moment, squinting as she let her eyes adjust to the sudden glare.

At the opposite end of the barn, Whit stood, with his back to her, scooping oats into a bucket.

"Whit?"

At the sound of her voice, he glanced over his shoulder. The surprise in his expression quickly gave way to a frown. Turning away, he scooped up oats. "Didn't mean to disturb you. Just wanted to get the stall ready, so I could put up the horses."

Taking a deep breath, she forced herself forward. "Grady was disappointed that you left. He wanted to help."

His hand faltered for a moment, then he set his jaw and shoved the cup down into the barrel, scooped up oats. "Figured it was best if I stayed away."

Tears burned her throat. "Best for who, Whit?"

"Grady. You."

"Grady doesn't want you to stay away." The tears pushed higher and she swallowed them back. "Neither do I."

With a groan, he sagged forward, bracing his hands on the edge of the barrel, and dropped his head between his arms. "I don't want y'all hurt, Melissa. If

I stick around, there'll be trouble. Mike'll see that there is.''

"My father has no control over my life."

He pushed from the barrel and whirled, his face taut with anger. "How can you stand there and say that, when he holds the deed to your land? He could call the loan just like that," he said with a snap of his fingers. "If he did, where would you and Grady go, what would happen to you then?"

"We'd manage."

He snorted a breath. "You'd manage," he muttered, and paced away, dragging a hand through his hair. He dropped his hand and swung back around to face her. "Let me tell you what it's like for a single woman, trying to raise a child on her own. You'll work sixteen hours a day trying to keep a roof over your head and food on the table. And while you're working your fingers to the bone, your son will be parked with friends or neighbors or whoever else the hell you can get to keep him. There won't be any money for doctor bills or braces or sport uniforms. You'll be damn lucky if you can make the bills each month, much less have any left over for extras."

She kept her gaze on his, knowing she'd just heard Whit's life story. "That was what your life was like before your mother married Buck."

"You're damn right it was," he said angrily.

"Can you honestly tell me that you wouldn't have chosen that life over the one Buck offered you?"

He opened his mouth, then closed it to scowl. "You're missing the point."

"No," she argued. "I think you are. My son's and

my happiness is worth a hundred times more to me than any material possessions my father might provide for us.''

''I'm talking about survival here, not happiness.''

She opened her hands. ''What is one worth without the other?''

When his scowl only deepened, she took a deep breath. ''I understand what you're trying to tell me, Whit. I really do. But you need to understand something, too. There was a time in my life when I thought I couldn't make it on my own. I lacked the courage to even try. And because I was a coward, I allowed other people to control my life, to make my decisions for me.''

''Your father?''

''Him…and others.'' She dropped her gaze, not wanting to discuss the past any longer. But she owed Whit an explanation for things her father had said. If not the whole truth, at least the part she felt she could safely share.

Lifting her head, she met his gaze. ''I never knew that my father had told you to stay away from me or that he forced you to leave town.''

''He didn't force me. Leaving was my choice.''

Tears burned her eyes as she experienced again the rejection she'd felt when she'd discovered he'd packed up and left without so much as a word to her about his plans. With it came the anger, the resentment, as well. ''You could've told me you were leaving. I think I deserved that much from you.''

''Tell you?'' he repeated. ''Hell, I tried every way

I knew how! I must've called your house a hundred times or more.''

She shook her head. ''You never called.''

''I didn't say I'd *talked* to you. I said I *called*. Y'all's housekeeper always answered the phone and said you weren't there.''

She felt the blood drain slowly from her face. ''She…she never told me.''

''I didn't figure she had, since you never returned a one of my calls. That's why I sent the letters.''

''What letters?''

''The letters I wrote to you,'' he said in frustration. ''When I went to see your father, it was to ask for your hand. He let me know in no uncertain terms that not only would he not give us his blessings, he would do everything within his power to see that I never saw you again. My plan was to go to Wyoming, cowboy for awhile, try to save up some money so we could buy us a place and make a good start together.''

She pressed a hand to her mouth to force back the emotion, unaware until that moment that Whit had wanted to marry her and had told her father so.

''When you never wrote back, I decided it was time to head home and find out what the hell was going on.''

She dropped her hand to stare. ''You came home? But…when?''

He turned away, dragging a hand over his hair. ''Hell, I don't know. A couple of months or so after I left, I'd guess. I was on a ranch in Wyoming and stuck out in a line shack miles from civilization, with nothing but a horse for transportation. First chance I got, I lit out for home.'' He stopped and looked back over his shoulder at her. ''That's when I found out you'd married Matt.''

She dropped her gaze, unable to face the accusation in his eyes. ''I thought you had left for good. That you were never coming back. Nobody at the ranch knew where you were, and when I asked Matt, he claimed he didn't know, either.''

He turned slowly to face her, his eyebrows drawn together in a frown. ''Matt knew where I was. I talked to him before I left town. Even gave him the address where I could be reached.''

''But he said he *didn't* know,'' she insisted.

He stared at her a long moment, as if refusing to believe his friend would do such an underhanded thing to him, then turned away, jamming his hands into his front pockets and kicking at the loose hay on the floor. ''Can't say as I blame him. I probably would've done the same damn thing, if I thought it meant I might have a chance with you.''

Tears welled in her eyes. ''No, Whit. You never would've lied for your own gain. You're much too honest a man to stoop to such low measures.''

At the opposite end of the barn, he stopped in the open doorway and braced a shoulder against the frame, his gaze on something in the far distance. He remained silent so long, she was sure he had nothing left to say to her.

''So where do we go from here?'' he asked after a moment.

She dragged a sleeve beneath her nose. ''I—I don't know.''

"Before your daddy showed up, we were working toward being friends again."

Choked by tears, she nodded. "My father's visit didn't change that. Not for me, anyway."

He angled his head around to look at her. "Do you mean that?"

She sniffed and lifted her chin. "Of course, I do. My father doesn't control my life. Not anymore."

He held her gaze a long moment then turned to look into the distance again. "I've still got the horse to train. Mike's not going to like me being around."

"That's his problem."

"What about Grady? If Mike should try to cause trouble, I don't want the boy hurt."

That he would consider her son's feelings above his own touched her heart in a way that little else could. "Neither do I. But Grady and my father have never been close. If given the choice, Grady would choose a friendship with you over a relationship with his grandfather."

"He shouldn't have to choose."

"No, but if forced, that's the choice he'd make."

Heaving a sigh, he pushed away from the door frame. "I guess I better get that stall ready, so I can bring the horses in."

"Do you need any help?"

He shook his head. "No. You go on back up to the house. I can handle things here."

She turned to leave, then stopped. "Whit?"

"Yeah?"

She glanced over her shoulder and met his gaze. "I hope we can always be friends."

Six

The next morning Grady and Melissa were sitting at the kitchen table eating breakfast when Melissa heard the sound of a truck approaching. Hearing it, too, Grady bolted from the table and ran to the back door to peer out.

"It's Whit!" he cried, and slapped open the screen door.

Tossing aside her napkin, Melissa hurried after him. "Grady, wait! You've still got on your pajamas!"

He kept running, his bare feet all but flying over the dew-dampened grass. With a sigh of defeat, she followed.

"Hey, Whit!" Grady called, waving a hand over his head. "Can I ride Molly?"

Whit stopped and waited for the boy to join him. "I suppose so."

"But he's not dressed," Melissa said breathlessly as she reached them.

Whit gave Grady a slow look up and down. "That's definitely not an outfit a cowboy would wear. But I doubt ol' Molly will care. I'll put a halter on her and bring her out to the corral. Wait over there by the gate."

Grady took off like a shot. Heaving another sigh, Melissa followed.

"Now you do exactly as Whit says," she instructed as Whit led Molly from the barn.

"Ah, Mom," he complained. "I know how to ride a horse."

"You've been on the backs of exactly two," she reminded him sternly. "And they were ponies, not horses, and both were tied to a walker at the county fair."

He gave his pajama bottoms a cocky hitch, as if the ponies he'd ridden were wild broncs fresh from the range. "I rode 'em, didn't I?"

Rolling her eyes, she said to Whit, "He doesn't have much experience with horses."

"He'll do fine," he assured her.

He draped the lead rope over his shoulder and scooped Grady up, swinging him onto the mare's back.

"Hold on here," he instructed as he closed Grady's hand around a fistful of mane. Plucking the lead rope from his shoulder, he looked up at Grady. "Ready to ride, cowboy?"

His face flushed with excitement, Grady bobbed his head.

Whit strode off, with Molly plodding along behind him. Melissa watched them make two laps. When they passed by, beginning the third, she felt confident enough to leave the two alone. "I need to go back and do the dishes," she called to Whit. "When Grady's through riding, will you send him up to the house so that he can get dressed?"

He tipped his hat in acknowledgment. "Will do."

She shifted her gaze to Grady. "And you mind what Whit says. I don't want you getting hurt."

"Ah, Mom," he complained. "I'm not a little kid."

"Yes, you are. You're *my* little kid."

"Okay," he mumbled, obviously willing to agree to anything so long as he was allowed to ride.

Satisfied, she turned for the house.

"Want to see how fast Molly can run, Grady?"

She spun back around. "Whit Tanner! Don't you dare make that horse run with Grady on her back."

Grinning, he pointed his finger at her like a gun and squeezed off a shot. "Gotcha."

Thankfully, Melissa's father stayed away from her ranch and the friendship she and Whit had pledged to each other slowly began to grow. Grady seemed to worship the ground Whit walked on and trailed him around like a puppy, bombarding him with a zillion questions. Whit answered each one with a patience Melissa found amazing.

Things were improving in the barn, as well. Molly

had the desired effect on War Lord, and the stud had begun to settle down. Whit had managed to get a halter on him and had even led him around the corral several afternoons in a row. He'd also been able to groom him, an achievement Whit insisted was Molly's doing, as War Lord had watched him groom Molly and had discovered that having his coat brushed was nothing to fear.

But Whit hadn't attempted to load him into a trailer yet, a fact that Melissa was eternally grateful for. She knew that once War Lord became transportable, Whit would no longer have a reason to come to her house every day.

And she would miss his daily visits more than she was ready to admit.

Sighing, she dropped her chin to her hand and stared out the rear workroom window at the gnarled oak tree that shaded her studio. She knew that she and Whit could never be any more than friends. Whatever chance for happiness they'd had ended with her marriage to Matt.

"Melissa?"

Startled, she turned to find Whit standing in the door of her studio, his hat in his hands.

She offered him a guilty smile and stood. "Sorry. You caught me daydreaming."

"No shame in that," he assured her as he stepped inside. "I just wanted to let you know that I'm cutting out early today. I've got to meet Ace and the others at a lawyer's office in Tanner's Crossing to sign the papers to settle Buck's estate."

Aware of the tenuous relationship between Whit

and his stepfather, she lifted a brow in surprise. "Buck included you in his will?"

He snorted a breath. "You knew Buck better than that. If he'd left a will, he wouldn't have named me in it. Since he didn't, his estate has to be split equally among his heirs."

Hiding a smile, she folded her arms across her breast. "Well, I guess there is justice, after all."

He shook his head. "I've already told the others I want no part of anything that was his. The only reason I'm going is so they can settle the estate and get on with their lives."

That he would refuse to accept what must amount to a small fortune didn't surprise Melissa. Not when the gift came from a man he held so little respect for and even less affection.

"Will we see you tomorrow?" she asked, changing the subject.

"Bright and early. I promised Grady he could ride Molly. He's trying to get in all the riding time he can before he has to leave for his grandparents'."

Reminded of Grady's annual trip to Matt's parents', Melissa sighed. "He doesn't want to go. Which is nothing new," she added. "It's a battle I fight every year. Matt's parents live in a retirement community in Georgetown and there is no one his age for him to play with. The Jacobses have forgotten how to keep a little boy entertained, if they ever knew at all."

Whit tipped his head in acknowledgment. "They never seemed to have much time for Matt when he was a kid. But with Matt gone now, Grady's all they've got left. I imagine they're lookin' forward to his visit more than ever.''

''Yes, but I wish Grady wasn't kicking up such a fuss about going. It makes me feel guilty for sending him.''

Whit lifted a shoulder. ''It's only for a week. I doubt he'll die from boredom in that length of time.''

''Not to hear him tell it,'' she said dryly, then shook her head and forced a smile. ''But school doesn't end for another week. Maybe in that length of time, a miracle will happen and he'll have a change of heart.''

''There's always hope,'' he said, then ducked his head as if he had something else to say but was hesitant to say it.

''Was there something else?'' she asked helpfully.

''Well, yeah,'' he said and looked up at her. ''I don't want you to think I'm trying to stick my nose in your business, but I was thinking about the property taxes that you mentioned.''

She stifled a shudder at the reminder. ''What about them?''

''Do you happen to know if Matt ever applied for an agricultural exemption?''

Frowning, she looked at him curiously. ''Not that I'm aware of. Why?''

''Well, if you were to run some cattle on the place, you could apply for an exemption on your taxes. It wouldn't help with those due now, but it would take a chunk out of those you'll owe in the future.''

She smiled, but shook her head. ''I appreciate the

advice. I really do. But I can't afford to buy any cattle right now.''

"You wouldn't have to," he was quick to tell her. "I could lease the land from you and bring some of my cattle over here. I've got more than I can adequately graze right now and was going to have to sell a few, which I really don't want to do. Not with the market being down like it is. If I bring 'em over here for a while, I can hold on to 'em until the price runs back up.''

She eyed him suspiciously. "Are you doing this just to help me out?''

He held up a hand, his thumb tucked against his palm. "I swear I'm not. It's a win/win deal for us both. You get the tax advantage, without all the hassle, and I get to keep my cattle.''

The law offices of McGregor, White and Wilcox took up the entire third floor of the Tanner bank building in downtown Tanner's Crossing. The three lawyers and their thirty-odd employees had handled the Tanners's legal affairs ever since Buck had taken over the reins of the Tanner fortune more than forty years before.

Judging by the richly paneled wood walls and mahogany and leather furnishings, Whit figured the lawyers had managed to keep their fair share of that wealth.

The conference room where the meeting took place was an elongated room with one full wall of windows that overlooked the town square. Framed degrees filled one of the shorter walls; the opposite held an antique mahogany buffet, complete with a massive silver coffee service fit for a king. Opposite the wall of windows, built-in bookcases stretched from floor to ceiling and were filled with leather-bound books, each containing the word ''law'' in the title imprinted on its spine.

Whit sat alongside Ace at the massive conference table that ran the length of the room. Woodrow, Ry and Rory sat across from them. McGuire, the lawyer chosen to preside over the meeting, sat at the head of the table.

Each of the brothers had a tall stack of legal documents stacked in front of him, awaiting his signature. At the lawyer's instruction, Ace, Woodrow, Rory and Ry picked up the pens placed alongside the documents and began signing their names.

Whit nudged Ace's elbow. ''I told you I didn't want anything of the old man's,'' he whispered.

His gaze focused on the legal document he was signing, Ace said absently, ''Too bad. It's yours. Sign your name, so we can all go home.''

Whit set his jaw and snatched up the pen. ''Fine. I'll sign my name, but that doesn't mean I'm accepting a thing.''

After signing the last document, Ace rose and extended his hand to the lawyer. ''We appreciate all the work you and your firm put into taking care of this for us.''

McGuire stood, too, as did the others at the table, and shook Ace's hand. ''It's always a pleasure to do business with the Tanners.'' He shifted his gaze to include the other brothers and added, "If our firm can be of service to you in the future, just give us a call."

After the documents were properly witnessed by two of the firm's clerks, there was nothing left to do or to say. Whit was the first out the door.

Ace caught up with him in the parking lot and slung an arm over his shoulders as Whit strode for his truck. "Appreciate you coming, Whit."

"I wouldn't have, if I'd had a choice," he returned.

Chuckling, Ace gave him a pat on the back. "Appreciate it just the same." When they reached Whit's truck, Ace held the door as Whit climbed inside. "Have you finished breaking Melissa Jacobs's horse yet?"

Whit shook his head. "No, but I'm making progress. Probably will try puttin' a saddle on him first of next week."

"How's Melissa doing?"

He lifted a shoulder. "All right, I guess. Money's tight, but she seems to be managing."

"Rory mentioned that you and her son were in the store the other day."

Ace's comment won a scowl. "Does Rory tell you about every customer who walks through his door?"

Biting back a smile, Ace shook his head. "No, but seeing you with a kid in tow was newsworthy enough to mention. Especially since you outfitted the boy in clothes."

"I was keeping an eye on him while Melissa was at a craft sale in Austin." He lifted a shoulder. "Since he was going to be hanging around with me at my barn all day, I figured he needed boots and jeans to save the wear and tear on his own clothes.''

''Uh-huh,'' Ace said, then laughed when Whit's scowl deepened. ''Listen, tomorrow's Maggie's birthday and Ry and Kayla are planning a little get-together for the family at the ranch. Nothing fancy. Just ice cream and cake. Why don't you bring Melissa and her son out? I know everyone would enjoy seeing her.''

''I don't know,'' Whit said uncertainly. ''She doesn't seem to do much socializing.''

''All the more reason to bring her.''

''I'll give it some thought,'' was all Whit was willing to commit to.

''Four o'clock,'' Ace said, and dropped his hand from his door. ''See you then.''

Saturday morning when Whit arrived at Melissa's, he was feeling more than a little stressed. Due to the amount of time he was putting in at Melissa's working with War Lord, he wasn't getting nearly enough sleep, a loss that contributed greatly to the amount of stress he usually felt.

But his stress that morning wasn't the fault of lack of sleep. He had two things to do this day and felt inadequate to accomplish either. The first, he hoped Melissa could help him with. The second, he was totally on his own.

Determined to ease at least one of his worries, he approached the house before going to the barn. As was his habit, he avoided the front door and went around to the back. Although he'd been inside Melissa's house on several occasions, he felt more at ease in the kitchen than any other room. He supposed it was because the kitchen lacked any memories of Matt. There were no pictures of his old friend scattered around. No personal items to remind Whit that Matt had once called the place home.

Melissa answered his knock. Her smile warm, she opened the door wide. "Come on in. I was just about to have a cup of coffee. Care to join me?"

Whit dragged off his hat and followed her inside. "Sounds good." He laid his hat on the table, then slid onto a chair.

Melissa set a mug of coffee in front of him, then sat opposite him, cradling a mug between her hands. "Grady's still asleep," she said as if she needed to explain the boy's absence. "I let him stay up late last night, watching a movie."

"He can ride whenever he wakes up. Just send him on down to the barn when he's ready." Frowning, he picked up a spoon and stirred his coffee, trying to work up the nerve he needed to address the first of his worries. "I need some advice," he began uncertainly.

Her brow knitted in concern, she set her mug down. "Is something wrong?"

Shaking his head, he set the spoon aside and wiped a hand down his mouth. "Not exactly. You see, today is Maggie's birthday. She's Ace's wife," he explained, unsure if Melissa knew Ace had married.

"I know. I met her at Macy's grand opening."

He dropped his gaze to his mug and nodded.

"Well, the family is planning a get-together over at the ranch to celebrate and I need to take a present."

When she didn't say anything, he glanced up and saw that she was trying hard not to smile. Scowling, he slumped down in his chair. "Hell, I don't know anything about what women like. I was hoping you could give me a few tips on what I might buy her."

"I'm sure I can. But it'll help if you can tell me a little about her."

"She's studying to be a nurse. Is nuts about Laura, the baby of Buck's she and Ace adopted. She's had kind of a hard life. Was taken away from her mother and raised by foster parents. I don't think she ever knew who her dad was. She was married once before. From what Ace told me, her ex treated her pretty bad." He lifted a shoulder. "That's about it."

"Does she have any hobbies? Any interests?"

"Not that I'm aware of, though she could be a concert pianist for all I know. From what I've seen, she pretty much devotes all her time to raising the baby and keeping Ace in line. And she doesn't mind cooking for a crowd. Before she and Ace married, she cooked for all the hands who worked on the ranch."

She looked away, her lips pursed in thought. "A devoted mother and wife and she likes to spend time in the kitchen," she said, thinking out loud. "That offers several possibilities."

Standing abruptly, she motioned for him to follow her. "Let's go out to the studio and see what we can find."

Whit grabbed his hat and followed. Once inside the studio, he hung back while she dug through boxes.

"What do you think about something like this?" she asked. "She could put a picture of the baby in it or perhaps a picture of Ace."

He studied the frame she held. "I don't know," he said, after a moment's consideration. "What do you think?"

"I think she will love it," she assured him. "But she'll like it even better if we add something to it, to make it especially hers."

She dug through the box and lifted out another frame. "Like this," she said.

He read the name on the crocheted piece inside the frame then looked at her in confusion. "Madison? How does that make it special for Maggie?"

"Not *this* particular frame," she assured him. "I can crochet another doily with the name Tanner or Laura on it. Either of those names would mean something special to Maggie."

"Yeah," he said, looking relieved. "How about doing the name Tanner? That way it could stand for all three of them. Ace, Laura and Maggie."

"Perfect," she said as she pushed to her feet. "I'll get my thread and crochet hook and start on it right now."

"Will you have time to finish?" he asked in concern. "The party starts at four."

She gave his arm a distracted pat as she passed by him on the way to the door. "No problem. I've made so many of these, I can probably whip one out in less than three hours."

Whit followed her outside. "Uh, Melissa. There's one more thing."

She stopped and turned, a brow lifted in question. "What?"

He dropped his gaze and studied his hat. "Well... uh...Ace thought you and Grady might...well, you might like to come to the party, too."

"Oh," she said, looking surprised.

"It's nothing fancy," he was quick to tell her. "Just ice cream and cake for the family. You don't have to go, if you don't want to. Ace just thought you might—well, enjoy getting out for a while."

She hesitated a moment longer, then smiled. "He's right. I would."

"If you want, I could come by and pick up the present on my way to the party. Y'all could ride with me, if you want."

She looked at him doubtfully. "Are you sure that's not too much trouble?"

"Not a bit. Say, about three?"

A slow smile spread across her face. "We'll be ready."

Later that afternoon as they approached the patio where the party was to take place, Melissa wished that she was six years old and could slip her hand into Whit's as Grady had. There was something intimidating about seeing the Tanner men gathered in one place. All four stood guard over an electric ice cream freezer. The slow whine of its motor signaled that the ice cream was almost ready. The women were noticeably absent, but a baby sat on a quilt, within easy reach of the men, and was busily filling a pail with colorful plastic blocks.

Ace was the first to spot the new arrivals and broke away from the group to greet them. Smiling, he extended a hand to Melissa.

"Glad you could join us."

"Thanks for inviting me."

His smile softening, he brushed the tips of his fingers across her cheek. "You doing okay?"

The concern, as well as the gesture, was so like Ace. Even as a teenager, he'd always had a tender heart.

"Yes," she assured him. "I'm doing fine."

"And who's this little guy?" he asked, shifting his gaze to Grady.

"Watch it," Rory warned from behind him. "He doesn't take too kindly to comments about his size."

Grinning, Ace hunkered down in front of Grady. "No offense meant. I'm Ace. What's your name?"

Taking a step closer to Whit's side, Grady mumbled a barely audible, "Grady Jacobs."

"Did you know that I've known your mama since she was no bigger than my little girl."

"How big is your little girl?"

"Little but growing up way too fast," Ace replied, then he rose and offered Grady his hand. "Want to meet her?"

Grady looked up at Whit as if to make sure it was all right.

With a nod, Whit released his hand. "We'll catch up with you in a minute."

Grady slipped his hand into Ace's. "What's your daughter's name?" he asked as the two walked off.

"Laura."

"How old is she?"

Chuckling, Melissa watched them cross to the baby. "Ace is going to wish he'd never befriended him. Grady will wear him out with all his questions."

"Not Ace," Rory said. "He loves kids."

"Any one ready for a birthday party?"

All eyes turned to the patio door as Kayla stepped through carrying a platter with a towering cake. Maggie, Elizabeth and Macy followed, with plates, bowls and spoons.

And the party began.

Two hours later there was nothing left of the cake but a slim wedge of icing, the last of the ice cream was a puddle of milk in the bottom of the can and those who had consumed it all were sprawled around the patio in various stages of sleep. Ace lay stretched out on the quilt, his head resting in Maggie's lap and Laura asleep on his chest. Woodrow and Elizabeth sat on the glider, their eyes closed and their heads and shoulders braced together to hold them upright. Rory had claimed the hammock beneath the trees and swung slowly with Macy curled against his side. Grady—tireless, as always—was playing ball with Ace's dog, Daisy, in the field behind the house.

A light breeze ruffled the leaves in the surrounding trees and birds chirped from high branches. The only other sound to break the peacefulness was the occasional spurt of laughter from Grady, and Daisy's excited yaps.

It was a warm, lazy scene, one that Melissa would normally have enjoyed. But with Whit sitting in the chair next to hers, there was no way she could relax. She was much too conscious of Whit's hand inches from hers and the way his fingers dangled from the end of the chair's armrest. His skin was tanned from hours spent in the sun and calloused from years of hard work. Some women might find their roughness unappealing, but to Melissa they were beautiful, even mesmerizing. Though she was aware of the amount of strength in them, she knew there was a softness there, as well. She'd seen the gentleness with which he handled the horses and the care he displayed when he dealt with Grady.

And she remembered the feel of those hands on her.

Woodrow stood suddenly. "If I sit much longer, I'm going to petrify. Or, worse, start licking the ice cream freezer. I think I'll run over and check on my goats. Had three sets of triplets this morning." He turned and shouted to Grady, "Hey, Grady! Want to go and see my baby goats?"

Caught in mid-throw, Grady wheeled to gape. "Shoot, yeah!" he cried, then dropped the ball, Daisy forgotten, and turned to his mother. "Can I, Mom?"

Laughing, she said, "Yes, I suppose."

Woodrow, Elizabeth and Grady loaded up into Woodrow's truck and left, promising to return within an hour. The disturbance aroused Ry.

Yawning, he looked at Whit. "Forgot to tell you. That stone you ordered for your mother's grave arrived yesterday. You might want to check and make sure it was what you wanted.''

''I think I will,'' Whit said, then glanced over at Melissa. ''Want to go with me?''

Since Grady had left with Woodrow, she had no reason to remain behind. ''I guess so.''

Standing, Whit stretched then draped an arm at her waist as if it was something he did every day and guided her from the patio. But Melissa felt the weight of his arm like a ring of fire around her waist.

His steps unhurried, he led her up the hill behind the house and to the family cemetery. Enclosed by an iron fence, the cemetery held the remains of several generations of Tanners. Melissa remembered attending the graveside services of Buck's first wife here. She couldn't have been more than three or four at the time, but she had a vivid memory of standing at her father's side and watching as each of the Tanner brothers filed solemnly by the grave and dropped a rose onto their mother's casket. She hadn't realized the extent of their loss at the time, but she remembered that each had been crying, which had saddened her.

Whit moved directly to his mother's grave, which lay to the right of Buck's. Though the grave itself was years old, the fresh clods of dirt packed around the pink granite tombstone denoted the marker's newness. Carved into the stone were the words, ''Lee Grainger Tanner, Devoted Mother whose memory will linger long with those who knew and loved her.'' This was followed by the dates of her birth and death.

Dropping his hand from Melissa's waist, Whit

knelt and smoothed a hand across the carved letters forming her name. Melissa watched his movements, sensing the love and devotion with the stroke of his fingers.

"It's pretty, isn't it?"

"Yes," she said quietly. "It's a lovely stone."

"Buck put one up when she died. It was gray, depressing. Had her name and dates on it, but that was it. I thought she deserved better." He ran a finger over the roses carved into the two uppermost corners. "She loved flowers. Once when I was kid, I picked her a bouquet from a neighbor's yard. Mrs. Carver's. An old spinster with nothing better to do than take a daily inventory of her blooms. She knew immediately that they were missing and figured I was the culprit. She called Mom and told her that I'd stolen flowers from her garden. Mom was so proud of the bouquet that I'd given her, she couldn't bring herself to punish me. Instead, she baked Mrs. Carver a pie and had me deliver it."

Touched by the sweetness of the story, Melissa laid a hand on his shoulder. He reached up and covered it with his.

"I miss her," he said sadly. "She's been gone almost thirteen years, but not a day goes by that I don't think about her."

"You must have loved her very much."

He slowly rose and pulled her hand down to hold in his. "More than she probably ever knew. I was never very good at expressing my feelings."

"She knew," Melissa assured him. "A mother knows those kind of things without being told."

He glanced her way. "Grady loves you."

She smiled softly. "I know."

"Does he ever tell you so?"

She lifted a shoulder. "Not as often as he did when he was younger."

"He should."

"It isn't necessary. I know that he does. He shows me in ways that are sometimes much more meaningful than hearing the words."

Intrigued, he led her to sit with him on a stone bench beneath a live oak tree and held her hand on his thigh. "How?"

She laughed softly. "I've received my share of bouquets he's pulled from my garden."

He grinned sheepishly. "Guess I'm not the only one guilty of stealing flowers."

"Flowers were meant to enjoy. I'm sure your mother derived a great deal more pleasure from the ones you picked than Mrs. Carver would have if they'd remained in her garden."

"What other kinds of things does he do?"

"Unexpected kisses. A gift of a particularly interesting bug he finds. Sometimes it's nothing more than a smile."

"You're lucky to have him. He's a great kid."

"Thank you. I think so."

Growing thoughtful, he turned his gaze to stare into the distance. "Does he miss Matt?"

His question caught her totally off guard and had her tensing. She inhaled in a long breath, then quietly released it. "Yes," she replied honestly, then added, "Though not as much as you might think."

He angled his head to look at her curiously. "What do you mean?"

She averted her gaze, uncomfortable discussing Matt with him. "He misses having him around the house. His presence. But Matt didn't spend much time with him, so he doesn't miss doing things with him."

"I suppose that's sorta how I feel about Buck. When I was living here on the ranch, we never had much of a relationship, but I always knew he was there. Not necessarily physically, as he was seldom at home. But I always knew that he would come back eventually."

She nodded in understanding. "The first month or so after Matt died, Grady would ask when he was coming home. I had explained death to him, so he understood that Matt was never coming home again. But it was as if he would forget and think Matt was simply away for several days."

"Do you miss him?"

Startled by the question, she glanced at him then dropped her gaze to their joined hands.

He gave her fingers a reassuring squeeze. "I'm sorry. I had no right to ask you that."

"No. It's okay." She took in another deep breath, unsure how to respond without revealing how tenuous her and Matt's relationship had been.

"I miss his presence," she finally said.

Seven

By the time they returned home from the party, it was after dark and Grady had fallen asleep on the seat, between Whit and Melissa, his head resting against Whit's shoulder.

When Melissa moved to wake him, Whit laid a hand over hers.

"Don't," he said quietly. "Poor guy's tuckered out. I'll carry him inside."

With a nod of assent, Melissa hurried ahead to unlock the back door. Once inside, she switched on the light over the sink, then led the way to the stairs. In Grady's room, she whipped back the covers, tugged off his boots, then plucked a pair of pajamas from his chest of drawers. While Whit sat on the edge of the bed holding him, she eased Grady out of his clothes and into his pajamas. As she withdrew, she winced at the dirt that smeared his cheek.

"I'll get a wet cloth and wash his face," she whispered.

"Don't," he said, shaking his head. "A little dirt won't hurt him."

The mother in her wanted to argue, but she moved aside, watching as Whit shifted him onto the bed.

Stepping back, he slipped an arm around her waist and stood with her for a long moment, watching Grady sleep. It was such a simple act, yet Melissa couldn't remember ever having shared this experience with anyone before. The bedtime ritual had always been hers alone, one that Matt had never cared to participate in.

"Do you think he's settled in for the night?" Whit whispered.

She choked a laugh. "If he wakes up before noon, I'll be surprised."

Chuckling, he turned her for the door. At the top of the stairs, he dropped his arm from her waist and followed her down. She knew that once they reached the kitchen, he'd probably leave, and she wasn't ready for him to go. Not yet. The day together had been wonderful and she wasn't ready for it to end.

"Would you like something to drink?" she asked, hoping to delay his departure.

He caught her hand and pulled her around. Startled, she braced her hands against his chest. The light over the sink didn't provide much illumination, but it was more than enough for her to see his eyes as well as the intent in them.

Framing her face within his hands, he stroked his thumbs along the ridge of her cheeks. "I've been wanting to do this all day."

Mesmerized by the huskiness in his voice, she asked, "What?"

He pulled her face to his. "This."

As his lips touched hers, she melted against him, knowing that the day spent with him had built to this moment. Or perhaps the need had been gathering force since the last kiss they'd shared. She'd spent hours thinking about that kiss, playing it over and over through her mind, trying to assess its meaning, weighing its importance, comparing it to the ones they'd shared when they were involved before.

Seven years stood between them, seven long years without so much as a word exchanged. After that length of time, kissing him should have seemed strange to her, awkward. Oddly, it felt natural. Right.

With her hands braced against his chest, her palms registered every beat of his heart, rose and fell with each breath he took. She stored each away as a precious memory to savor later.

Wanting to touch him, to have him closer, she lifted her hands and pushed her fingers through his hair. Lacing them behind his head, she parted her lips and mated her tongue with his.

With a groan, he backed her up against the wall. "Oh, God, 'lissa," he murmured as he rained kisses over her face. "It's been so long."

The need in his voice had her clinging tighter to him and when he found her lips again, she responded to it with one that equaled his. As she slid deeper and deeper into the kiss, she brought her hands to his cheeks, holding his face to hers, giving and taking with an abandon she hadn't experienced in years.

His hands seemed to be everywhere, stroking her arms, gliding along her neck, knotting in her hair. But when he slipped them beneath her blouse, her breath snagged in her lungs and burned. Deepening the kiss, he slowly moved his hands upward, the tips of his fingers grazing her flesh, until he reached her bra. Fanning his fingers across the lace that covered her, he cupped his hands over her breasts, molding their shape within his palms.

Groaning, he pushed a knee between hers and pressed his groin against her. Heat flooded her womb at the intimate contact.

He held himself there a moment, then began to stroke her breasts. "You're bigger," he murmured against her lips. "Fuller than before."

She gulped, her nipples knotted and aching for more of his touch. "Pregnancy," she managed to say. "Sometimes it does that to a woman."

He stiffened and she knew it was the mention of her pregnancy that caused the change. Wishing desperately that she could take the words back, she said tearfully, "I'm sorry."

Shaking his head, he dragged his hands from beneath her blouse and wrapped his arms around her, held her close. "No. That's a part of your life that I'm going to have to deal with." He pulled back to look at her and cupped a hand at her cheek. "It's just so damn hard to think of you being with another man. I loved you, 'lissa. More than you'll ever know."

Choked by emotion, she covered his hand with hers.

With a sigh, he slowly dragged his hand from beneath hers. "It's late. I'd better go so you can get some sleep."

She watched him leave, her heart breaking, wishing she had the right to call him back.

Long after Whit had left, Melissa sat on the window seat in her bedroom, staring out into the night, her arms hugged around her knees, her mind too troubled for her to consider sleep.

I loved you, 'lissa. More than you'll ever know.

Her heart ached anew each time she thought about what Whit had said. She'd always known that he'd loved her. But when he'd left without a word of explanation, she'd begun to doubt his love, until she'd finally questioned whether he'd ever loved her at all.

Moaning, she dropped her forehead to her knees. If only she'd believed in him, trusted him to come home to her, she never would've married Matt. It was desperation that had sent her running to Matt, and fear that had forced her to accept his proposal. When Whit had left, she'd been young and scared and living under the rule of her father's iron hand. She'd been weak, a coward, and had let others control her life.

But she wasn't a coward any longer. Her independence and trust in herself had been hard-earned, but she'd come out of the experience with a greater confidence and a determination to never rely on anyone ever again.

Then Whit had reentered her life.

Sighing, she lifted her head to stare out the window. She was falling in love with him all over again. And that terrified her, as there were so many obstacles that stood in the way of them finding happiness together. First and foremost was their past, something he was obviously having a hard time dealing with. And there was—

"Mom?"

She snapped her head around to find Grady standing in the doorway. She quickly scraped the heels of her hands across her face to wipe away the tears, then swung her legs to the floor and opened her arms. "What's wrong, baby?" she asked in concern as she gathered him close.

Rubbing his eyes, he leaned into her, resting his head on her shoulder. "Where's Whit?" he asked sleepily.

She stroked a hand over his hair, realizing how attached her son had become to Whit.

"Probably at home by now, and fast asleep," she said softly, then pressed the back of her hand to his forehead. "Do you feel sick, sweetheart?"

Yawning, he shook he head. "Uh-uh. I woke up and had to go to the bathroom. Is Whit coming back tomorrow?"

"I hope so," she said with a sigh, then rose and took his hand, wanting to put an end to his questions. "Come on. I'll walk you to your room and tuck you back into bed."

The next week passed in a blur of activity. It was the end of the school year and there was a party at

Grady's school that Melissa had to bake cookies for, as well as attend. And Matt's parents were picking Grady up Saturday morning for his annual week-long visit, which meant she had laundry to do and a suitcase to pack. To complicate matters even more, one of her best customers had placed a last-minute order for fifteen personalized graduation gifts.

All of which had kept her busy at the house or in her studio. Whit came every day to work with War Lord, as was his habit, but once he realized how overworked she was, he kept a respectful distance. He even entertained Grady at the barn, which kept her son out of her hair, an act of kindness she would be eternally grateful for.

Still, by the time Saturday rolled around, she was a wreck. Grady had already thrown one fit that morning about having to go and stay with his grandparents, which had increased Melissa's level of stress. She would have gladly kept him at home with her to make him happy, but she knew how much Matt's parents looked forward to having him stay with them.

By 9:00 a.m. she had his bag packed and ready by the front door, and was in the kitchen making a fresh pot of coffee, when it occurred to her that the house was unusually quiet.

Suspicious, she set the carafe down and headed for the foot of the stairs. "Grady?" she called. "Why don't you come down and help me make coffee for Peepaw and Mimi?"

When he didn't respond, she set her jaw and climbed the stairs, knowing he was probably hiding in his closet. "This isn't funny, Grady," she warned.

* * *

Whit dumped half the oats into War Lord's feeder, then moved down to the next stall and poured the remainder into Molly's. He paused a moment to scratch Molly's ears before heading back to the feed room to return the bucket to its hook.

Out of the corner of his eye, he caught a flash of movement outside and turned to look out the barn door. A grin slowly spread across his face when he saw Grady flying down the hill from the house, his arms and legs pumping like pistons.

As Grady grew nearer, Whit started for the door, planning to meet him there. He jerked to a stop when he got a good look at the boy's face and saw the tears streaming down his cheeks. "Grady," he murmured, and broke into a run.

They met at the barn door and Whit scooped him up. Sobbing, Grady flung his arms around Whit's neck and buried his face in its curve.

Gulping at the emotion that filled his throat, Whit braced a hand at the boy's back and held him close. "Hey, cowboy," he said softly. "What's wrong?"

"Don't l-let Mom make m-me go," he begged.

Frowning, he cupped a hand behind the boy's head and moved to sit on a bale of hay. "Don't let her make you go where?"

"Peepaw's and M-Mimi's."

It was hard to understand the boy, what with him crying so hard, but Whit knew that today was the day that Grady was supposed to leave for Matt's parents' and figured the boy had to be talking about them.

"Why don't you want to go to see your grandparents?"

Sobbing, Grady clung tighter. All Whit could make out of his muffled reply were the words "stay here with you."

That the boy would rather stay with him than go to his grandparents did something to his chest, making it ache. Unsure what he should say, he rubbed the boy's back.

"I imagine with your dad gone," he said, "your grandparents get pretty lonely."

When Grady only cried harder, Whit searched his mind, trying to think of something that might distract the boy from his tears.

"Did you know that your dad and I were friends when we were about your age?" He didn't wait for a response, but kept right on talking. "Yep. I used to hang out at your grandparents' house all the time. Course they still lived in Tanner's Crossing back then. Had this great big house over on Pecan Street with a huge backyard. Your dad and I used to play baseball there nearly every day after school."

Chuckling softly, he shifted Grady to a more comfortable position on his knee. "I remember one time I was pitching and threw him a curve ball. Was sure he'd miss it by a mile. But he put wood to leather and sent that ball sailing high and long. Busted out the window in one of the upstairs baths. I thought your grandmother was going to have a stroke."

When he realized that Grady's crying had slowed and he seemed to be listening, he went on. "She lined us up and read us the riot act, threatening to whip us both, if one of us didn't confess. Your dad told her that I broke it and she made me mow their grass for a month to pay for replacing the window.''

Grady lifted his head slightly. ''Why did you take the blame? You coulda just told Mimi that Dad broke it.''

He lifted a shoulder. ''I figured I was guilty as he was, since I was the one to throw the ball. Besides, your grandmother probably would've come down a lot harder on him, being as he was her son.''

''She's never spanked me.''

Whit reared back to look at him. ''Have you ever broken one of her windows?''

''No.''

Whit tugged his handkerchief from his back pocket and pressed it to Grady's nose. ''Then she had no reason to. Blow,'' he instructed.

Grady blew, Whit wiped, then ordered Grady to blow again.

After he was done, Whit tucked the handkerchief back into his pocket. ''Do you ever play cards with your grandfather?''

Grimacing, Grady shook his head. ''No. We don't ever do nothin' but watch boring game shows on television.''

''You ought to challenge him to a game of Go Fish. He used to beat my socks off at least once a week.''

''Peepaw beat you?''

''Well, I was just a kid,'' Whit said defensively. ''I doubt he could beat me now.''

''I bet I could.''

Whit gave him a measuring look. ''Maybe. Maybe

not." He shook his head, chuckling. "I remember one time I bet him a dozen of your grandmother's famous chocolate-chip cookies that I could beat him two out of three games."

"Did you win?"

"No. And I had to mow their yard another week, before your grandmother would bake the cookies I needed to pay off my bet."

"Mimi sure was mean to you."

"Mean?" Whit repeated in amazement. "Heck, that lady was good as gold to me. Let me hang out at her house all the time and eat her food."

"Didn't your mom cook for you?"

"Sure she did. But she worked nights, which is why I was at your grandparents' so much. If not for your grandmother feeding me dinner, I probably would've have turned into a bologna sandwich, since that was all I knew how to make for myself."

"Grady Jacobs, I've been looking all over for you!"

Whit and Grady both looked up to find Melissa standing in the doorway, her face creased with worry and flushed from exertion. Giving her a silent look asking her not to come down hard on the boy, Whit stood, hitching Grady on his hip.

"We were just fixin' to head up to the house," he told her, then glanced at Grady and shot him a conspiratorial wink. "Grady came down to remind me to give Molly an apple every day while he was gone and we got to shootin' the breeze. Guess we forgot the time."

He set Grady on his feet, then ruffled his hair.

"Now you be sure and tell your grandparents hello for me. And don't worry about Molly," he added, with a wink. "I'll see that she gets that apple."

Confused, Melissa looked back and forth between the two, then extended her hand. "Come on, Grady. You'll want to wash up a bit before Mimi and Peepaw get here."

Grady slipped his hand into his mother's and walked with her from the barn. At the door, he glanced back over his shoulder and grinned at Whit. "I'll bring you some of Mimi's famous chocolate-chip cookies," he promised.

Smiling, Whit lifted a hand in farewell. "You do that."

Whit stayed busy at the barn, but he was aware of the Jacobs's arrival and was relieved to see that, when they left a little while later, Grady was riding in the back seat of their car.

Biting back a smile, he swung down from Molly's back, then unwound War Lord's lead rope from around the saddle horn. "Good job, Molly," he said praisingly, and gave the mare a pat. Though the stud still spooked a bit at being touched by a human, Whit shifted to give him a pat, as well. He'd noticed a marked improvement in the stud's attitude over the last couple of days. With Molly serving as post horse, Whit had managed to lead the stud around the corral, changing directions every so often in an effort to teach the stud to respond to changes in tension on his halter similar to those produced by a bridle and reins.

After hitching both horses to the fence, he began

to unsaddle Molly. Sensing he was being watched, he glanced over his shoulder and found Melissa standing by the gate. He tugged the saddle from the horse's back and started toward her.

"I saw that Grady got off," he said as he swung the saddle up to balance on the top rail of the fence.

"Yes," she said, and stepped closer. "And I want to thank you for whatever it was you said to Grady that convinced him to go. It would've broken their hearts if he'd refused to leave with them."

"I figured as much."

She tipped her head and looked at him curiously. "Exactly what did you tell him, anyway? Not more than fifteen minutes before they arrived, he informed me the only way I was going to get him in the car was if I hog-tied him and bodily threw him in."

Whit stifled a shudder. "I think I could've handled a temper tantrum easier than I could the tears." He scooped a brush from the tack box and began to brush Molly down. "He was pretty upset when he first showed up at the barn."

"Every year it gets harder and harder to persuade him to go. He swears there's nothing to do there, and that all the Jacobses do is sleep and watch game shows on TV."

He nodded as he swept the brush along Molly's back. "He mentioned that."

She lifted her hands helplessly. "I don't know what to do. I hate sending him when he obviously hates to go. But I know how much the Jacobses look forward to having him."

"They're going to have to take some of the heat off you."

"And how are they supposed to do that," she asked miserably, "when I'm doing everything I can to keep them from knowing that Grady doesn't want to visit them anymore?"

"It's their job to see that he enjoys the visits. If they were to put forth a little more effort, Grady wouldn't mind going and you wouldn't have a battle on your hands."

She lifted a brow. "Would you like to be the one to tell them that?"

"Probably won't need to. I gave Grady a couple of hints that might take care of the problem."

"Like what?"

"Like he should challenge his grandfather to a game of Go Fish. I figure, too, after telling him about his grandmother's chocolate-chip cookies, he's going to ask her to bake him some. Odds are, if he does, he'll end up with some flour on his nose."

"That was very clever of you."

He lifted a shoulder as he moved to Molly's opposite side. "Wasn't trying to be clever. Just couldn't stand the thought of him being miserable while he was gone."

"Neither can I, but I never would've thought to do what you did."

Growing thoughtful, he swept the brush along Molly's neck. "I guess with Grady gone, you won't be cooking supper tonight."

She folded her arms over her chest and gave him

a droll look. "Is that a hint that you'd like a free meal?"

Biting back a smile, he propped an elbow on the mare's back. "No. I was thinking more of offering you one. What would you say to going with me to Bubba's tonight and eating some barbecue?"

Her lips slowly turned up in a smile. "I'd say that sounds like a fine idea."

"About seven?"

"I'll be ready."

Bubba's was an institution in Tanner's Crossing. Buried at the end of a dirt road and snugged up to the bank of the Lampasas River, the restaurant did a thriving business. Though their menu was limited, the quality of food they served more than made up for the lack of choices. Barbecue was their specialty, but on Saturdays they pulled out the deep fryers and served up platters of golden-fried catfish, accompanied by heaping bowls of cabbage slaw and baskets filled with fried hush puppies. The recipes were Bubba's own, and he guarded them with his life.

Whit had chosen the restaurant with Melissa in mind, thinking the relaxed atmosphere and down-home cooking would be a welcome relief after the busy week she'd put in.

Bubba himself greeted them upon their arrival and seated them at a table by a window.

"This is beautiful," Melissa said, her gaze on the view of the river beyond the glass.

He opened his menu. "It's that, all right," he said as he studied it. "How does catfish sound?"

"As long as I don't have to cook it, I'll eat anything."

Chuckling, he set the menu aside. "Catfish it is, then."

When the waitress arrived, he placed their orders, then settled back, stretching his legs out beneath the wooden table, and smiled at her. "Did you finish the order for the graduation gifts?"

She heaved a weary sigh. "Yes, but barely."

"You could've just told the lady you didn't have time."

"And take a chance on losing a customer?" She shook her head. "No. I need the business too badly."

Leaning forward, he clasped his hands on the table, preparing to make an offer that had been building in his mind. "I know you've said you won't accept money from me," he began.

She held up a hand. "It's not just you. I don't want to borrow money from anyone."

"And I understand why you feel that way," he said patiently. "Even respect you for it. But I inherited a chunk of money from Buck that I have no intention of ever using. I could give you whatever you need to pay off your father and you can pay it back whenever you want. No notes. No liens. No pressure."

Smiling softly, she reached to cover his hands with hers. "You're sweet to offer, but my answer is still no."

Frustrated, he dragged his hands from beneath hers and braced them against his thighs. "Dang it, Melissa. I'm just trying to help you out."

"I know you are, and I appreciate it. I really do. But I'm determined to handle this on my own."

He scowled as the waitress appeared with their plates and waited until she left before offering one last comment. "I won't bring it up again," he promised, "but the money's there for the taking. If you change your mind, all you gotta do is give me the word and it's yours."

"Fair enough," she said as she picked up her fork. "Now eat before your food gets cold."

After helping Melissa into his truck, Whit climbed behind the wheel. "Would you mind if we ran by my place before I take you home?" he asked as he turned the key. "I've got a horse I need to doctor."

"No, that's fine."

With that decided, he turned the nose of his truck for his ranch. "Wonder what Grady's doing right now?" he asked after a moment.

Growing pensive, she turned her face to the passenger window. "I don't know, but whatever it is, I hope he's having fun."

He stretched an arm along the seat behind her and gave her neck a reassuring squeeze. "He'll be fine."

"I hate that I made him go," she said guiltily.

"Want to give him a call?"

She snapped her head around to look at him. "Now?"

He plucked his cell phone from its holder on the dash and offered it to her. "Might as well."

She took the phone, quickly punched in the number, then lifted it to her ear. After a moment she said, "Hi, Ruth. It's Melissa. How's everything going?"

As she listened, she gave Whit a thumbs-up sign. "If it won't interrupt the game," she said in response to a question. A moment later a smile bloomed on her face and he knew Grady was on the phone.

"Hi, sweetheart. Are you having fun?" As she listened to his reply, her smile slowly faded. "Well, sure, sweetheart. I understand. Be a good boy and mind your grandparents."

"What did he say?" Whit asked as she disconnected the call.

"He said he was having a great time but had to go because he and Richard were in the middle of a card game."

More than a little relieved at the news, Whit returned the phone to its cradle on the dash. "So why the sad face?"

"I'm not sad."

He reached over and flipped down the visor in front of her, exposing the mirror. "Now tell me that face isn't sad."

Grimacing, she pushed the visor up. "I'm not sad. It's just that…" She lifted a hand and let it drop. "I miss him and thought he'd miss me, too."

"I guess the Jacobses are doing a better job at entertaining Grady than I am you. Maybe I should've challenged you to a game of Go Fish instead of taking you to dinner."

She sputtered a laugh as he pulled up in front of his barn. "Thanks, but I'll take dinner at Bubba's over a game of Go Fish any day of the week."

Grinning, he shut off the engine. "Want to wait here? This won't take long."

She reached for the door handle. "No, I'll go with you."

He led the way inside the barn and paused to turn on the lights. "It's the mare over there," he said, pointing to a stall on his left. "I'll get the medicine."

Left alone, Melissa wandered over to the stall and looked inside. The horse stood with her hips pressed against the wall, her head hanging low. A mean-looking gash ran in a jagged line from the top of her right foreleg to her knee.

"Pretty gruesome, isn't it?"

She glanced over at Whit as he slid back the stall door, then followed him inside. "Yes, it is. What happened to her?"

Murmuring softly to the horse, he hunkered down in front of her and began to clean the cut. "Not sure. She belongs to a buddy of mine. Said he saw her one morning standing by the fence, her leg covered in blood." He took a jar of cream and began to smear it over the cut. "Could've gotten into some barbed wire. Or a wild dog might've attacked her." He lifted a shoulder as he recapped the jar of cream. "Whatever the case, he couldn't afford to take her to a vet, so he brought her over here." He pulled a syringe from his shirt pocket and turned the needle up, thumping a finger against the barrel as he pushed in the plunger to release any air bubbles.

She winced as he pushed the needle into the horse's flesh. "What's that for?"

"Antibiotic to ward off any infection."

Rising, he capped the needle. "All done. I'll put these things away and we'll be ready to go."

Melissa followed him out of the stall, then waited outside the barn for him. Darkness had settled completely and the moon was out, a circle of silver light surrounded by glittering stars. Hugging her arms beneath her breasts, she closed her eyes and inhaled deeply of the night air.

She felt the weight of Whit's arms slip around her from behind and leaned back against his chest.

"It's a beautiful night," he said quietly.

Opening her eyes, she stared up at the sky. "I love this time of year. Warm days and cool nights. This is my idea of heaven."

"Sure beats August when the thermometer hovers around a hundred degrees twenty-four hours a day. Makes me yearn for Wyoming."

Reminded of the time he'd spent away, she lowered her gaze and looked around. "How long have you lived here?"

"About three years. I bought the place not long after I moved back to Tanner's Crossing."

"Was it because of me that you stayed away?" she asked hesitantly.

He rubbed his cheek against hers. "Partly. Didn't seem to be any reason for me to come back."

She folded her arms over his. "But you eventually did."

"Yeah. I missed home. Texas, really. Hot as it gets here, it's still the best place to live in my estimation."

She angled her head to look up at him. "I'm glad

you came back. I don't know what I would've done, if you hadn't."

"You'd have managed."

Laughing softly, she bussed a quick kiss on his cheek. "You're either blind or lying through your teeth. In either case, I appreciate the vote of confidence."

Dropping his arms from around her, he caught her hand. "Would you like to see the house? It's not much, but it's home."

"I'd like that."

"We can walk, if you want. Give us a chance to work off some of our dinner."

Chuckling, she shifted her hand within his to lace her fingers through his. "I definitely need to do that."

They started off at a relaxed pace, swinging their joined hands between them. The night was quiet, with only the sounds of nature to disturb the peacefulness. As they approached the house, Melissa's steps slowed even more.

"Oh, Whit," she murmured, charmed by the sight of the simple stone structure. "It's beautiful."

"It suits me," he said as he guided her up the steps.

On the porch, she stopped and looked around as he unlocked the door. "Was the house here when you bought the property?" she asked curiously. "Or did you have it built?"

He pushed the door wide. "I built it. Most of it, anyway," he added quickly. "I hired out the electrical and plumbing." Placing a hand low on her back, he ushered her inside, flipping on a light as he closed the door behind them.

He tossed his hat onto a chair near the door. "I haven't done much with the inside," he said, obviously embarrassed by the sparsely furnished rooms. "Never can seem to find the time."

She turned a slow circle, awed by the craftsmanship in the bead-and-board walls and the stone fireplace. "I can't believe you did all of this yourself."

"Woodrow helped with the woodwork," he admitted. "He's got a knack with things like that. And Rory mixed mortar and hauled rock, while I laid the stone."

"You're lucky to have them," she said.

"Yeah. I suppose I am." He cleared his throat, then gestured toward an open door. "Would you like to see the bedroom?"

She turned to look at the darkened door, wondering if he was inviting her for more than just a tour. Taking in a deep breath, she slowly released it.

"Yes, I would."

Eight

With Whit's hand at her back, guiding her, Melissa crossed the den and entered his room.

Once inside, he brushed past her and crossed to switch on a lamp beside the bed.

When he turned, he lifted a hand. "This is it. Not much to it, really. Just a place to sleep."

"It's perfect," she assured him.

He ducked his head, then lifted it a fraction to look at her from beneath his brow. "I've never brought a woman here before."

Her heart melted at the admission. "I'm honored to be the first."

He held out a hand, his palm up in invitation. Her hands shaking a bit, she moved to place hers in his. He pulled her to him and slipped his arms around her waist. "I want to make love to you, 'lissa," he said quietly. "Here in my bed."

Emotion rose to fill her throat at the meaningfulness in the simple statement. Forcing a swallow, she nodded. "I want that, too."

He pulled back to cup a hand at her cheek and looked deeply into her eyes. "I want you to know that there's never been another woman for me but you."

She wanted to tell him she felt the same about him, but feared he would never believe her if she did. Instead she wrapped her arms around his neck and pressed her lips to his. He quickly deepened the kiss and she closed her eyes, with a sigh, giving herself up to the moment, to him.

All too soon, he withdrew and sat on the side of the bed. Tugging her over to stand between his spread knees, he looked up at her as he reached for the top button of her dress. With a slowness that had her trembling, he worked his way down the front, releasing each button in turn. When he freed the last one, he folded back the sides, exposing her body to his gaze.

Almost reverently, he placed a finger at the center closure of her bra, then dragged it down, leaving a trail of fire along her stomach until he reached the waist of her panties. Pressing his lips just below her navel, he slipped his fingers beneath the elastic band of her panties and eased them down her legs.

She held her breath as he opened his hands over her stomach, fighting the urge to cover the stretch marks that marred her skin.

"Was he a big baby?" he asked as he traced the faint lines with his thumbs.

A smile trembled on her lips at the concern in his voice. "Not really. Seven pounds, two ounces."

He pressed his lips against a mark, then smoothed a finger over the moisture he'd left there as he looked up at her. "It's hard to believe you could carry a baby at all. You're so small."

She wrinkled her nose. "I looked like a whale and waddled like a duck. It wasn't a pretty sight."

Standing, he pushed the thin straps of her sundress over her shoulders and let them slide down her arms. "I bet you were beautiful."

Her breath caught as he unhooked her bra, then shuddered out of her as he tossed it aside. "Whit," she said weakly.

He fitted his hands at her waist and covered her mouth with his. "We're going to take this slow," he murmured against her lips. "Real slow."

But slow wasn't what Melissa needed or wanted. Her skin was already on fire, her breathing shallow. Impatient to have him as naked as she, she pulled his shirttail from the waist of his jeans.

"Next time," she promised breathlessly. "Right now I want you."

Chuckling, he ripped open his shirt, then sank down on the side of the bed and toed off his boots, stripped off his jeans. When his clothes lay in a pile on the floor next to hers, he looked up at her and opened his arms.

Melissa fell into them with a groan, forcing him back on the bed.

He rolled with her, until she was beneath him, then found her mouth with his. His kiss was passionate, his hands electrifying and she was sure that if he didn't take her then and there, she would die of want.

She tore her mouth from his. "Whit, please," she begged.

"Are you sure you're ready?"

"Yes. Please."

His gaze on hers, he shifted to straddle her and stroked his thumb along her folds, spreading them before guiding his sex to her opening. Bracing his hands at either side of her head, he slowly lowered his hips.

As he pushed inside, she arched high, gasping, clutching at his hips and holding him to her while her body adjusted to his size. When she could breathe again, she moved her hips against his, urging him to give her more and more of his length.

With a low moan, he dropped his mouth to her breast and took her in, suckling in rhythm with the thrusts of his hips against the curve of hers. Blinded by the heat that burned behind her eyes, she squeezed them shut and clung to him as pleasure danced playfully just out of her reach.

"Whit," she begged.

Shifting his mouth to hers, he slipped a hand beneath her hips and lifted, then thrust hard. She tore her mouth from his, sobbing his name as pleasure ripped through her in waves. As her body pulsed wildly around him, she felt the tension that stiffened his body, the spasm of muscle, and nearly wept as the warmth of his seed spilled inside her.

Breathing hard, he collapsed against her and buried his face in the curve of her neck. "You okay?"

Sated, she wound her arms around him and all but purred, "Never better. How about you?"

Chuckling, he rolled to his side and gathered her close. "Ask me that again in the morning. Right now all I can feel are my toes."

Melissa hadn't expected to be there to ask Whit the question, but when she awoke the next morning, she was still in his bed.

And he was sprawled beside her.

Realizing that this was the first time they'd ever spent the night together, she curled a hand beneath her pillow and watched him sleep.

He is so unbelievably handsome, she thought, and had to ball her hand into a fist to keep from touching him. And so irresistibly cute when asleep. Obviously accustomed to having the bed to himself, he had claimed over three-quarters of the space. He slept on his stomach, with one hand buried beneath his pillow and the other fisted loosely on top. His hair was sticking up in all directions and a dark stubble of beard shadowed his jaw.

Absolutely and irrevocably precious, she decided, and reached to smooth a wayward lock of hair from his forehead.

"Good mornin'."

Startled, she jerked her hand back, then smiled and cuddled close when she realized he was awake. "Good morning."

He hooked an arm around her and dragged her closer. "Hungry?"

"Not especially. Are you?"

"I could eat a whole cow and be lookin' for more when I was done."

Laughing, she ruffled his hair. "Obviously you can feel more than your toes this morning."

He smoothed his hands up her back, then down again. "I can feel a whole lot more than my toes." He squeezed her buttocks. "And I sure like what I'm feeling."

The heat that poured through her was fast and intoxicating. Smiling, she ran a finger down his chest. "You don't feel so bad yourself."

He groaned as her finger glided over his sex. Draping a leg over hers, he hauled her up against him. With his arms wrapped tightly around her, he buried his nose in her hair. "I love you, 'lissa. I don't think I ever stopped."

Her heart seemed to stop. Slowly she pushed back to look at him. "I—I don't know what to say."

"You don't have to say anything at all. I just wanted you to know."

Her eyes filling with tears, she rested her head on the pillow opposite his. "Show me how much you love me."

He flipped back the covers and dragged her over on top of him. "Now that's something I can do."

And he did. He showed her in ways that Melissa didn't know were possible. By the time he finally entered her, she was half wild with need...and had never felt so completely and utterly adored.

* * *

Later that day Melissa sat in her studio, making a list of supplies she needed. It was difficult keeping her mind on her work, since she knew that Whit was in the corral working with War Lord. She finally gave up and went to the window to peer out. Simply seeing him was enough to turn her weak with need.

He was the most virile, yet sweetest man she'd ever known, traits he'd proven to her repeatedly over the past twenty-four hours. The kindness and wisdom he'd displayed with Grady when he'd persuaded him to go to his grandparents'. Inviting her to dinner when he'd known she'd be lonely with Grady away. The tenderness, as well as the passion, he'd offered to her while they were making love. The understanding he'd freely given when he'd told her that he loved her and she hadn't been able to tell him that she loved him in return.

But she did love him. There was no way she could deny her feelings for him. But she couldn't say the words to him. If she shared her feelings with him, she opened up the potential for a relationship, a future together.

And she knew that was impossible. There were still secrets that lay between them. Things that Whit was totally unaware of.

As she watched him climb up into the saddle, she held her breath, waiting for War Lord to bolt or to buck or to do something equally dangerous in an effort to throw him off. The horse did rear once, then spun in a dizzying circle, but Whit remained in the saddle.

Could she tell him everything without destroying his love for her? she wondered as she watched him ride the horse along the side of the corral. He seemed to have come to terms with her marriage to Matt. She doubted he and her father would ever be close, but that really didn't matter as she and her father had never been close. And he seemed to sincerely care about Grady.

But would he still, when he learned the truth?

Unsure of the answer, she turned away from the window and returned to the desk.

As she picked up her pen again, she told herself to give things time. There was a chance that nothing would become of her and Whit's relationship. He claimed to love her, but maybe what he felt for her was nothing more than lust. If that's what it proved to be, she'd deal with it. She'd dealt with losing him before.

But she wasn't going to tell him everything and take a chance on hurting the most important person in her life.

Her son.

Melissa was a pro at blocking things from her mind that she didn't want to think about. She'd had years of practice in which to hone the skill to perfection. Thus, it was easy for her to greet Whit with a smile when he came to the studio later that afternoon.

"Are you done for the day?" she asked.

He dragged off his hat and mopped the sweat from his brow. "And then some. But I rode him."

Her smile widening, she rose from her stool. "I know. I saw you. How did he do?"

"Stiff. Tried to pitch a couple of times. All things considered, though, I'd say he did all right."

"How long before you think he's ready to sell?"

He scratched his head as he crossed to her. "Hard to say. A couple of weeks. Maybe a month. You'll want him reining better before you put him in a ring. It'll give him time to muscle up some, too. He's got a hay belly on him. Now that I'm riding him, he'll lose that pretty quick."

"Wow," she said, surprised that things were moving along at such a fast pace. "It seems as if it was only yesterday that you started working with him."

He shot her a wink. "Time flies when you're having fun."

She blushed to the roots of her hair, knowing very well what he was referring to.

Chuckling, he dropped a kiss on her mouth. "You sure are cute when you're embarrassed."

"I'm not embarrassed."

He dragged a knuckle along her cheek. "Could've fooled me."

She swatted at his hand. "I'm not."

"Uh-huh," he said, then changed the subject. "Have you heard from Grady today?"

She winced at the reminder. "No, and I'm trying really hard not to call him."

"Probably wise. Hearing your voice would probably make him homesick."

"Well, that certainly makes me feel better," she said dryly.

Laughing, he slung an arm around her shoulders and headed her for the door. "I know just the thing to get your mind off missing Grady."

"And what would that be?" she asked, though she had a feeling she knew what he would suggest.

He shook his head. "I'm not telling. That would ruin the surprise." He dropped his arm from around her. "Go on up to the house and change clothes. Something you don't mind getting messed up," he added. "I'll put the horses up and feed 'em. When you're ready, come on down to the barn."

The surprise Whit had planned for Melissa very nearly backfired on him. He'd thought it would be fun to return to one of the places they'd frequented when they'd dated before. But when he drove up to the lake on the Tanner ranch and killed the engine, she took one look at the tree where he'd carved their initials and burst out in tears.

He immediately cranked the engine. "We don't have to stay here," he said, thinking the place held nothing but bad memories for her. "It was probably a dumb idea. We can have our picnic somewhere else."

She patted the air between them, while trying to get her emotions under control. "No. It's okay." She pressed her hands to her cheeks and took a deep breath. When she released it, she turned to look at him. "I can't believe you remembered."

He hooked an arm over the steering wheel and reached to thumb away a tear that hung on a lash. "How could I forget? This place was special for us.

Probably the one we came to most often. As I recall, I didn't have much money back then. Couldn't afford to take you on any real dates like the other guys did their girls.''

"It didn't matter," she assured him. "This was so much better."

"So you don't mind that I brought you here?"

"You couldn't have taken me anywhere that I would've liked any better."

"Then let's get that blanket and spread out our picnic before it gets dark."

Together they gathered their supplies and carried them to the tree that bore their initials. After Whit spread the blanket beneath it, Melissa began to unload the sack that held their food.

"Wine?" she asked, holding up a bottle. "I don't remember you picking that up when we stopped for groceries."

"I didn't intend for you to."

She lifted a brow. "Is there anything else you didn't intend for me to know about?"

He shrugged and went back to stacking wood for a campfire. "Maybe. You'll just have to wait and see."

Within minutes he had a small blaze going and had stretched out by her side on the blanket. The sun was quickly slipping below the horizon, taking with it its heat, but the fire promised to keep them warm.

He lifted a hand. "The view's better down here."

Smiling, Melissa placed her hand in his and allowed him to pull her down by his side. She nestled close, resting her head in the curve of his arm and looked up at the first stars to appear in the sky. "Do you remember the day you carved our initials in the tree?" she asked quietly.

"Yeah. Do you?"

"Yes. It was the first time you told me you loved me."

He rolled to his side and laid a hand on her stomach. "And the first time we made love."

She turned her head to look at him and covered his hand with hers. "This tree holds a lot of special memories for us."

"Yeah," he agreed. "And I'd like to add another one." He waited a beat, then said, "I want to marry you, 'lissa."

Stunned, for a moment she could only stare. "Oh, Whit," she said uneasily. "There's so much to consider."

"I'm not saying we have to get married tomorrow. I know some folks might find fault with you marrying so soon after Matt's death."

"It's not the gossips I'm worried about, it's... Grady."

He nodded grimly. "I've given that some thought myself. I had a stepfather, so I know there's a strong possibility Grady might resent my presence in his life. But I've grown to love him and hope that someday he'll feel the same way about me. I want you to know that I'll do everything within my power to see that he never has cause to hate me the way I hated Buck."

Before she could think what to say, how to respond, he went on, "You don't have to give me an answer now. I know this is all pretty sudden. Just promise me you'll think about it.''

She released the breath she'd been holding, feeling as if she'd been given a reprieve. "Okay."

Seemingly satisfied with her answer, he sat up and rubbed his hands together. "Now how about some of those hot dogs?"

She sat up, too, though not with the same level of enthusiasm as he had. "That sounds good."

While Whit fished the hot dogs from the bag, Melissa looked around. "Have you seen my purse?" she asked. "I want to call and check on Grady."

"I think it's still in the truck."

"Right," she said, and crossed to the truck to retrieve it. Returning, she sank down by the fire and pulled out her cell phone. "Looks as if he called me first," she said, recognizing the number of the missed call on the screen.

"Must not have heard the ring," he said as he skewered a wiener onto a wire hanger. "Call him back."

She lifted the phone to her ear. "I will. But first I'm going to listen to the message he left. They may have been planning to go somewhere."

But the recorded voice wasn't Grady's, it was his grandmother's. Melissa listened a moment, then clapped a hand over her mouth, her eyes filling with tears.

Whit glanced her way and frowned. "What's wrong?"

She held up a hand to silence him, listening, then leaped to her feet, stuffing her purse into her bag.

"It's Grady. He's had an accident. They've taken him to the hospital."

Whit dropped the hanger and shot to his feet. "In Georgetown?"

She nodded, tears streaming down her cheeks. "I've got to go. He'll need me."

He grabbed her arm and hustled her to the truck. "I'll take you."

After helping her inside, he climbed behind the wheel and gunned the engine. Grabbing his own cell phone from the base on the console, he punched in a number as he raced the truck across the pasture. "Rory," he said into the receiver. "It's Whit. I've gotta make this fast. I left a campfire burning by the lake at the Bar-T. I need you to douse it, then grab Ry and Elizabeth and meet me at the hospital in Georgetown. Grady's been in an accident."

When Whit pulled up in front of the emergency entrance, Melissa jumped from the truck and ran into the building. Whit was a step behind her.

"Grady Jacobs," she said to the receptionist. "I'm his mother."

The receptionist quickly checked the records. "They've already taken him to surgery."

Melissa paled at the mention of surgery and Whit quickly slipped a hand around her waist to keep her from sinking to the floor.

"Where?" he asked.

"Down that hall to your right," the receptionist said, pointing. "You'll find his family in the waiting room."

Keeping a firm hold on Melissa, Whit ran with her to the waiting room. As they entered, Ruth and Richard Jacobs rose, their faces creased with worry.

"Where's my baby?" Melissa sobbed. "What happened to him?"

Ruth buried her face in her hands, her shoulders heaving. Richard slipped an arm around her, comforting her. "He fell out of a tree," he explained, "and broke his arm. Got a pretty deep gash on his head. The doctor has him in surgery now."

Melissa flung an arm at the window. "But it's dark outside! What was he doing climbing a tree in the dark?"

Richard hung his head. "It wasn't dark when he went outside. The three of us were watching TV and I guess Ruth and I must have nodded off. When we woke up, Grady was gone. We had everyone looking for him. Searched for over two hours. One of the security guards finally found him down by the creek that runs alongside the golf course."

Melissa pressed her fingers to her lips. "Oh, God. My baby. My poor baby."

A commotion at the door had them all turning to see Rory, Ry and Elizabeth entering the room. Woodrow followed close behind.

Whit quickly updated them on what had happened. "He's in surgery now," he said in conclusion. "That's all we know."

"I'll go and talk to the nurse on duty," Ry said. "See what I can find out."

Elizabeth slipped an arm around Melissa's waist

and hugged her against her side. "He's going to be all right," she assured her.

"Melissa?"

Melissa snapped up her head to see Ry standing in the doorway, accompanied by a doctor dressed in surgical garb. She rushed forward.

"Is he okay?" she asked, her chin quivering.

The doctor nodded. "He came through the surgery just fine. The bone was shattered in two places," he explained. "We inserted pins to aid in the healing. The gash on his head took sixteen stitches to close, but there doesn't appear to be any damage to the brain.

"Grady lost quite a bit of blood, though, and is going to need a transfusion. Unfortunately, his blood type is AB negative and we don't have any on hand. We can request the blood bank in Austin to send us some, but we were hoping you have the same type and can serve as his donor."

"I'm O positive," Melissa said.

"What about Mr. Jacobs?"

"He's deceased."

Whit stepped forward. "I'm AB negative. I can give him blood."

"Good," the doctor said, looking relieved, then motioned for Whit to follow him. "The phlebotomist can take your blood and test it for compatibility while I finish up in surgery." He handed Whit a file. "Give this to the technicians and they'll get you set up. The lab is the third door on your right."

With a nod, Whit hurried down the hall. Within minutes he was stretched out on a gurney, a tourniquet wrapped around his upper arm. While he watched the slow stream of his blood flow through the tubing, he silently prayed that Grady would come through this no worse for wear.

"That's one lucky little boy," the phlebotomist said as she monitored the level of blood. "The odds of you having the same blood type as him are really high. Only one out of one hundred and sixty-seven people have AB negative."

"I don't care about the odds," Whit said impatiently, anxious to get back to Melissa. "I just want Grady to be all right."

With a nod, she eased the needle from Whit's arm. "We've got what we need," she said. Keeping a finger pressed against the vein to halt the flow, she quickly replaced it with a cotton ball and taped it into place. She handed Whit a cup filled with orange juice. "Lie right there for a few minutes and drink this juice," she instructed. "You might be a little light-headed. I don't want to take a chance on you passing out."

Whit turned the cup up and drained it. "Don't worry about me. Just make sure that blood is a match."

She turned for the door. "I'll be back in a few minutes to check on you."

Left alone, Whit glanced at the clock on the wall, willing the hands to move faster. He wanted to be with Melissa, to give her the support she needed. He knew that she was worried about Grady, and right-fully so. After just losing her husband in a tragic accident, he knew her concern for her son must be amplified a hundred-fold.

Impatient with the slow movement of the hands on the clock, he looked around the room and his gaze settled on the file the nurse had left on the counter.

The odds of you having the same blood type are really high.

He frowned, remembering the technician's comment. One in a hundred sixty-seven was the statistic she'd given. His frown deepening, he sat up and swung his legs over the side of the gurney. He waited a moment, giving the dizziness a chance to pass, then stretched an arm across the distance and nabbed the file. Pulling it to his lap, he flipped open the cover and scanned the information until he reached the date of birth listed. He noted the month, day and year, then slowly counted back nine months in his mind.

His body tensed in denial.

"No," he murmured, not wanting to believe what it meant. But the truth was there in his hands.

Tossing aside the file, he strode from the lab and down the hall. In the waiting room, he stopped in the doorway. Melissa sat in a chair beside Elizabeth, her head bowed, her hands squeezed together against her lips. As if sensing his presence, she looked up and met his gaze. He watched the blood slowly drain from her face and knew it was true.

Grady was his son, not Matt's.

He spun and stalked from the room. He had almost made it to his truck when he heard Melissa's voice behind him.

"Whit! Wait!" she cried. "Let me explain."

He whirled to face her, his entire body shaking with rage. "And how do you plan to do that? He's my son, Melissa. *Mine,* and you never told me."

"I couldn't."

"It's not that hard. You open your mouth and say the words. It's that simple."

"It's not that simple," she replied, her temper flaring to match his. "You were gone when I found out I was pregnant. My father knew the baby was yours and was going to make me have an abortion. I tried to find you, but no one knew where you were, not even Matt."

"That's a lie. Matt knew where I was. Before I left, I told him where I was going and how to get in touch with me."

"If it's a lie, it's his, not mine. I was scared to death that my father would force me to have an abortion, so when Matt said he would marry me and would give the baby his name, I agreed."

Whit shot his fingers through his hair and paced away, then turned back to glare at her. "We've been together for over a month now. You could've told me at some point during that time that Grady was my son."

She shot the question back at him. "And what if I had? Do you have any idea how complicated this is? Grady thinks Matt was his father. How do I explain to him that *you're* his real father?"

"What about me?" he cried. "I have a part in this, too. Now that I know I have a son, do you expect me to just walk away and pretend he doesn't exist?"

She dropped her face to her hands and shook her

head. "I don't know," she said wearily. "I don't know what either of us should do."

"Well, I can tell you this much. I'm not walking away. That's my son in the hospital, and I'm not turning my back on him like my father and stepfather did me. You can decide when and how you want to go about telling him, but he's gonna know that he has a father who loves him."

Nine

————

Work was as good a catharsis as any for pain and one that Whit had relied on time and time again in the past. Work had seen him through the death of his mother and, later, the loss of Melissa to Matt, and he planned to use it to work through this current tragedy, as well.

Over the past week he'd cut, raked and baled a field of hay. It now lay in the field, ready to haul to the barn. Loading it onto the trailer was a backbreaking, mindless chore, but it provided a way for Whit to keep his hands busy while he waited to hear from Melissa. He'd put the burden of deciding when and how to tell Grady he was his father on her shoulders, and he didn't feel the least bit guilty for having done so.

The lie was hers to deal with, not his.

He'd called the hospital every morning and every night to check on Grady's progress, plus left his cell number with the nurses on Grady's floor in the event his condition took an unexpected change for the worse. But the boy was doing well.

Ry had made two visits himself to check on his progress and had reported to Whit that Grady was going to be fine. Grady complained about the restrictions that had been placed on his activity, but Ry had said that was normal for a boy Grady's age, who was used to running full-steam ten or more hours a day.

Whit didn't know what was normal activity for a six-year-old, since he'd been denied watching his son grow; yet another grievance to add to his growing list of reasons to be angry with Melissa.

He'd just heaved one last bale onto the trailer and was headed for the tractor, ready to haul the load to the barn, when he heard a truck approaching. Glancing toward the road, he recognized Rory's truck. He swung up onto the tractor seat, started the engine and headed for the gate, knowing Rory would wait for him there.

At the gate, he hopped down and thumbed back his hat, wiping a sleeve across his brow as Rory climbed down from his truck. "You're just in time to help unload," he told his stepbrother.

"In this heat?" Rory shook his head. "You're going to have to find yourself another sucker. I'm too old for this kinda work."

Chuckling, Whit hooked a boot on the top of the gate. "You were born too old for this kinda work. What brings you way out here?"

Rory dropped his gaze and lifted a shoulder. "Just thought I'd stop by and see how you're doing."

It was something one of his stepbrothers or their wives had done every day following Grady's accident.

"I'm okay. Just trying to stay busy."

"They released Grady about noon today."

Whit lifted a brow, unaware of the news. "I guess that means he's out of the woods."

"Ry said the doctor wouldn't have let him go home if there was any reason to keep him."

"I appreciate Ry keeping an eye on Grady. I'm gonna owe him big-time for all he's done."

Rory wiped a hand down his mouth, hiding a smile. "Oh, I imagine he'll think of a way to cash in on that debt."

Whit nodded grimly. "I'm sure he will."

"Listen, Whit," Rory said, growing serious. "I know this is none of my business, but I'm thinking if you and Melissa were to sit down and discuss this rationally, the two of you could work this thing out."

Scowling, Whit dragged his foot from the gate. "You're right. This isn't any of your business."

"Have you tried looking at this from her viewpoint?" Rory asked in frustration. "Personally, I think what she told you makes sense. You know Mike Grady as well as the rest of us do, so you know he would've done everything within his power to see that Melissa had an abortion. With you not being around to help her, she did the only thing she could and that was marry Matt."

Scowling, Whit dragged off his hat and braced his

hands on the gate. "I don't blame her for marrying Matt. It's the fact that she never told me that I had a son that I hold against her."

"And how was she supposed to do that when she didn't even know where you were?"

"I moved home three years ago. You can't tell me she didn't know that I was back in town. She found me easily enough when she wanted me to break Matt's horse."

"By the time you moved back, Grady was what? About three?"

"Close enough."

"Married and with a three-year-old child, who everyone, child included, thought was Matt's." Rory gave Whit a pointed look. "Now tell me the truth. If you were in her place, would you have rushed over and told a man you hadn't seen in four years that he was the father of your child?"

"Whether I would have or not isn't the point. She continued to live the lie."

"Come on, Whit," Rory said in growing frustration. "You know you love Melissa."

"I did. I don't know how I feel about her anymore."

Rory nodded gravely. "I guess I can understand how your feelings might be confused right now. You've had a hell of a shock. But don't let your pride and your anger destroy whatever chance you and Melissa and Grady have at becoming a family. You grew up without a father, so you know what it's like. And you had a stepfather for a time, though I doubt all stepfathers treat their stepchildren the way Buck treated you. Grady deserves to have both a mother and a father, a normal family life. You can do what you can to provide that for him, or you and Melissa can play a game of tug-of-war with the boy trapped in the middle and shuffle him back and forth between your two homes."

When Whit remained silent, Rory kicked at the dirt then turned for his truck. "The choice is yours," he conceded as he walked away. "I sure as hell hope you make the right one."

That night, Whit couldn't sleep. He prowled his house like a caged tiger, unable to shake free from all Rory had said. He kept telling himself that this mess wasn't his fault, that if Grady was hurt by any of it, it would be on Melissa's head, not his.

But his mind kept circling back to Rory's parting statement.

The choice is yours. I sure as hell hope you make the right one.

He didn't like thinking he had control over the situation. It was easier to believe that Melissa held all the strings.

Rory had placed another unpleasant thought in his mind when he'd suggested that Whit should consider Melissa's viewpoint. Alone, pregnant, probably scared to death. If her father had had his way, there wouldn't be a baby for them to fight over. Though Whit suspected Matt's reasons for offering to marry Melissa were selfish, in a way his friend had done him a huge favor. He'd provided Melissa a way to save Whit's son.

But Whit couldn't get past the fact that Melissa had seen him nearly every day for the past month and never once made an attempt to tell him the truth about Grady. Hell, he'd even proposed to her, promising to be a good father to Grady, and she hadn't even hinted that the boy was his.

He stopped his pacing, frowning as he tried to remember something she'd said. They'd been sitting by the campfire when he'd dropped the idea of marriage on her. When she hadn't immediately leaped at his proposal, he'd assumed it was because she was afraid of what people would say, what with her being so recently widowed.

It's not the gossips I'm worried about, it's…Grady.

He dropped his head back with a groan as he remembered her reply. She hadn't been worried about herself. Her first concern had been for her son…*their* son. And even if she'd wanted to tell him about Grady right then and there, he hadn't given her the opportunity. He'd dived right into telling her what a good father he would make, then closed off the opportunity for further discussion by asking her if she was ready for a hot dog.

A hot dog, for God's sake! There she was probably stressed to the max trying to figure out a way to tell him he had a son and he'd offered her a damn hot dog. What a fool he'd been! What a blind, stupid, fool.

And he was sure, if he thought hard enough about it, there were other times she might've tried to tell him. It had always struck him as odd that when she mentioned Matt, it was never as ''Grady's father'' or ''my husband.'' He'd never heard her refer to him as anything other than Matt.

He dropped down onto the sofa and held his head between his hands. Rory was right when he'd said that Whit loved Melissa. He'd loved her from the moment he'd first laid eyes on her, and he loved her now. He was mad, hurt, angry, vengeful, but when he stripped away all those emotions, he was still very much in love with her.

Lifting his head, he looked at the clock on the kitchen wall. It was after midnight. Much too late to go to her house now to try to talk to her.

''Like hell it is,'' he muttered and headed for the door.

Melissa sat at the kitchen table, carefully dropping bits of glass over a square of clear glass. The image she'd traced onto the surface was that of an eagle caught in midflight, its wings spread wide. She had chosen ten different colors of tumbled glass to use to show the detail of the eagle and its feathers. When finished, she would frame the image in wood and it would be a grandmother's gift to her grandson for achieving his Eagle rank in Boy Scouts. Quite an accomplishment for any young man to make.

She leaned back to study the design, then tensed and cocked her head, sure that she'd heard a sound coming from upstairs. She waited, listening, but when she didn't hear the sound again, she sighed and scooped up another spoonful of tumbled glass, telling herself that it was her nerves making her hear things. She had checked on Grady less than a half hour ago and found him sleeping peacefully. With the pain medication the doctor had prescribed, it was unlikely he would wake again until morning.

And when he did, she'd probably still be sitting at the table, bleary-eyed and punchy from lack of sleep.

But going to bed was useless. She'd tried. Several times, in fact. But sleep continued to elude her.

A light tapping on the back door had her snapping up her head. She glanced at the clock, saw that it was after one, then gulped and turned her gaze to the door again. Fisting her hand around the tweezers she'd used while working with the bits of glass, she eased up from her chair and tiptoed to the door.

"Who's there?" she asked, trying to hide the tremble of fear in her voice.

"Whit."

Hope flared for a moment, then slowly faded, and she dropped her forehead against the door with a moan of disappointment. Considering the lateness of the hour, she doubted his visit boded well for her and she was too emotionally drained to endure another ugly scene. Lifting her head, she unlocked the door— but left the safety chain in place—and opened it a crack. "What do you want?"

"I need to talk to you."

"It's the middle of the night."

"I'm aware of the time. It's important."

She vacillated a moment, then with a huff, slid back the chain and opened the door. "Please keep your voice down," she said irritably. "I don't want Grady to wake up."

He dragged off his hat and stepped inside. "I didn't

come to yell at you again, if that's what you're worried about.''

She flopped down in her chair and snatched up the spoon, refusing to look at him. ''Then say whatever it is you came to say and leave. As you can see, I'm rather busy.''

''I'll do my best to keep it short.'' He pulled out the chair opposite hers and laid his hat on the table as he sat. ''How's Grady?''

''As well as can be expected.''

''Is he in any pain?''

Though she heard the concern in his voice, the worry, she kept her head down, refusing to respond to it. ''Some. The doctor prescribed medication for it.''

''I guess he's probably driving you crazy wanting to go outside and play.''

Pursing her lips, she pushed a stray piece of glass into the design. ''He's six years old. I'd worry if he didn't.''

''I'd guess you'd know more about that than I would. I've never spent much time around kids.''

She ignored the stab of guilt his remark elicited. ''Yes, I imagine I would.'' Anxious to send him on his way, she set her tools aside and lifted her head to look at him.

She immediately wished she hadn't. Dark circles shadowed his bloodshot eyes, a strong indication that he hadn't been sleeping any better than she had. Plus, his hair was mussed, his shirt wrinkled, and he looked as if he'd dropped at least ten pounds since the last time she'd seen him.

She balled her hand into a fist to keep from reaching out and smoothing the worry line that lay between his brow. "If you came to inquire about Grady's health, I've told you all I know."

"No," he said quietly. "That's not why I'm here."

Tears burned her throat and she fought them back. "Then what do you want, Whit? I'm really tired and would like to go to bed."

"I came to ask your forgiveness."

"Forgiveness?" she repeated, her anger spiking at the injustices she felt he'd heaped upon her. "For what? For getting me pregnant seven years ago and leaving me to deal with it alone? Or did you want to apologize for making me feel like a heel for never telling you you had a son?"

"All of that and more."

His answer was so unexpected that she could only stare.

He dropped his gaze and rubbed his hands slowly over the table. "It wasn't fair of me to demand that you tell Grady I'm his father. Though it hurts me that he'll never know, I realize now what kind of problems that would create for him." Shaking his head, he looked up at her. "And I don't want to cause any more problems for him. Or you, either, for that matter. I figure you've both had enough to deal with, as a result of losing Matt."

The tears that had burned her throat, pushed higher as she saw the pain in his eyes and realized the tremendous sacrifice he was willing to make to protect her son. "Maybe when he's older," she offered uncertainly.

"No. It wouldn't be right, no matter what his age. He's always thought Matt was his father and that's the way it needs to stand. But I would like to ask a favor of you."

"What?"

"I'd like to maintain a relationship with him, if you'll let me. I grew up without a father. I know how tough that can be at times. I won't push myself on him or anything like that. But we had sorta become buddies while I was working here. If he's willing to continue with that, I'd like to be his friend."

Unable to stop the tears that flooded her eyes, she wiped a hand across her cheek. "He adores you. Surely you must know that. He's nearly driven me crazy, asking if you were going to come and see him and begging me to call you."

He smiled softly as if hearing that pleased him. "I sensed he liked me."

"I'm so sorry, Whit," she said tearfully. "For everything. If there was a way I could make this any easier for you, for all us, I would."

"There might be one way you could."

She looked at him in confusion. "How?"

"Marry me. If I can't be Grady's father, let me be his stepfather."

She opened her mouth but couldn't squeeze a word past the emotion that filled her throat.

He reached across the table and covered her hand with his. "I love you, Melissa, and always have. I had to work my way through the anger and resentment before I realized that nothing has changed that.

If anything, I love you more for what you did to save my son.''

"Oh, Whit," she cried softly. "I never would've married Matt if I thought I'd had any other choice.''

"I know that. At least, I do now.''

Pulling his hand from hers, he rose and rounded the table. He dropped onto a knee at her side and took her hand in his. "Will you marry me, 'lissa?''

She tugged her hand from his and flung her arms around his neck. "Yes, yes, a thousand times yes! Oh, Whit, I love you so much.''

Groaning, he dragged her down to hold her against his chest, his heart. "And I love you, Melissa, and I love our son. I'm going to be the best dang stepfather Grady could ever want.''

Leaning back, she smoothed a hand over his hair and searched his face. In his eyes, she saw the sincerity, the honesty, the determination to be all those things...and so much more. "I know you will, Whit. You have a father's heart.''

"Mo-m-m-m!''

At the sound of Grady's voice, they both bolted to their feet and ran for the stairs and up to Grady's room.

She hurried to his bed. "What is it, sweetheart? Is your arm hurting?''

He shook his head. "I need to use the bathroom.''

She stooped to pick him up. "Okay. I'll take you.''

He shrunk away. "No. I want Whit to.''

"No problem, cowboy," Whit said, and scooped Grady up, being careful with his bandaged arm.

While the two crossed to the adjoining bathroom,

Melissa straightened Grady's covers and fluffed his pillow. When they returned, she quickly stepped out of the way, giving Whit room to lay Grady down again. After settling him against his pillow, Whit sank onto the edge of the bed.

"I need to ask you something," he said to Grady.

"What?"

Whit reached for Melissa's hand and pulled her to his side. "I want to marry your mom and I was wanting to know if that's okay with you."

Grady looked at him warily. "Does that mean you'll live with us?"

"I'd like for y'all to move to my place and live with me."

"Could Mutt be my dog?"

Chuckling, Whit nodded his head. "Yeah. I 'magine Mutt would think that was okay."

"Would you be my dad?"

Whit gulped, then slowly nodded. "If you want me to, I'd be proud to be your dad."

Grinning, Grady slid beneath the covers. "That'd be cool."

With tears brimming in her eyes, Melissa leaned down and placed a kiss on his forehead. "You better go to sleep now."

He closed his eyes. "Okay. 'Night, Mom."

"Good night, sweetheart."

She switched off the lamp and turned for the door, lacing her fingers through Whit's.

"I love you, Mom," Grady called after them.

"I love you, too, baby."

"Whit?"

He stopped in the doorway and glanced back over his shoulder. ''Yeah?''

''I love you, too.''

Gulping, Whit squeezed Melissa's hand. ''I love you, too, son.''

*   *   *   *   *

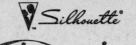

Silhouette Desire

Coming in December 2004

The Scent of Lavender
series continues with

Jennifer Greene's

WILD IN THE
MOMENT

(Silhouette Desire #1622)

The whirring blizzard, the cracking fire and their
intimate quarters had Daisy Campbell and
Teague Larson unexpectedly sharing a wild
moment. The two hardly seemed like a match
made in heaven...so why couldn't Daisy turn
down Teague's surprise business deal and
many more wild moments?

The Scent of Lavender

The Campbell sisters awaken to passion
when love blooms where they least expect it!

Available at your favorite retail outlet.

eHARLEQUIN.com

The Ultimate Destination for Women's Fiction

Your favorite authors are just a click away
at www.eHarlequin.com!

- Take a sneak peek at the covers and
  read summaries of **Upcoming Books**

- Choose from over 600
  author **profiles!**

- Chat with your favorite authors
  on our **message boards.**

- Are you an author in the making?
  Get advice from published authors
  in **The Inside Scoop!**

**Learn about your favorite authors
in a fun, interactive setting—
visit www.eHarlequin.com today!**

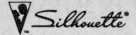

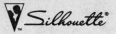

COMING NEXT MONTH

#1621 SHOCKING THE SENATOR—Leanne Banks
Dynasties: The Danforths
Abraham Danforth had tried to deny his attraction to his campaign manager, Nicola Granville, for months—although they *had* shared a secret night of passion. With the election won and Abraham becoming Georgia's new senator, would the child Nicola now carried become the scandal that would ruin his career?

#1622 WILD IN THE MOMENT—Jennifer Greene
The Scent of Lavender
The whirring blizzard, the cracking fire and their intimate quarters had Daisy Campbell and Teague Larson unexpectedly sharing a wild moment. The two hardly seemed like a match made in heaven…so why couldn't Daisy turn down Teague's surprise business deal and *many more* wild moments?

#1623 THE ICE MAIDEN'S SHEIKH—Alexandra Sellers
Sons of the Desert
Beauty Jalia Shahbazi had been a princess-under-wraps for twenty-seven years and that was how she planned to keep it. That was until sexy Sheikh Latif Al Razzaqi Shahin awakened her Middle Eastern roots… and her passion. But Latif wanted to lay claim to more than Jalia's body— and she dared not offer more.

#1624 FORBIDDEN PASSION—Emilie Rose
Lynn Riggan's brother-in-law Sawyer was everything her recently deceased husband was not: caring, giving and loving. The last thing Lynn was looking for was forbidden passion, but after briefly giving in to their intense mutual attraction, she couldn't get Sawyer out of her head… or her heart. Might an unexpected arrival give her all she'd ever wanted?

#1625 RIDING THE STORM—Brenda Jackson
Jayla Coles had met many Mr. Wrongs when she finally settled on visiting the sperm bank to get what she wanted. Then she met the perfect storm— fire captain Storm Westmoreland. They planned on a no-strings-attached affair, but their brief encounter left them with more than just lasting memories….

#1626 THE SEDUCTION REQUEST—Michelle Celmer
Millionaire restaurateur Matt Conway returned to his hometown to prove he'd attained ultimate success. But when he ran into former best friend and lover, Emily Douglas, winning over her affection became his number-one priority. Problem was, she was planning on marrying another man…and Matt was just the guy to make her change her mind.

SDCNM1104